Catherine Raws

Johann Wolfgang von Goethe

The Roman Martyr

SALZWASSER
VERLAG

Catherine Rawson Worsley, Thomas Worsley, Johann Wolfgang von Goethe

The Roman Martyr

Reprint of the original, first published in 1859.

1st Edition 2023 | ISBN: 978-3-37513-808-0

Verlag (Publisher): Salzwasser Verlag GmbH, Zeilweg 44, 60439 Frankfurt, Deutschland
Vertretungsberechtigt (Authorized to represent): E. Roepke, Zeilweg 44, 60439 Frankfurt, Deutschland
Druck (Print): Books on Demand GmbH, In de Tarpen 42, 22848 Norderstedt, Deutschland

THE

ROMAN MARTYR

A YOUTHFUL ESSAY IN DRAMATIC VERSE

BY

NOMINIS UMBRA.

WITH TRANSLATIONS &c.

BELONGING CHIEFLY TO THE SAME PERIOD

BY

THE EDITOR.

WILLIAMS AND NORGATE,
14 HENRIETTA STREET, COVENT GARDEN, LONDON;
AND
20 SOUTH FREDERICK STREET, EDINBURGH.
1859.

L'ENVOYE

THE EDITOR TO THE AUTHOR.

Gentle Heiress of a name
Known in arms and song to fame
Fear from me no critic blame.

Bathed once more by thy revealing
In the stream of youthful feeling
I too learn its magic healing.

Thanks! And may thy later sorrow
Balm from these sweet memories borrow
Breathed o'er many a happy morrow.

Notice.

The following Dramatic Essay was written before the year 1830.

ERRATA.

Page 6,	line 12,	*for*	mornful	*read*	mournful.
〃 43,	〃 3 and 4 from bottom,	〃	It	〃	If.
〃 46,	〃 12 from top.	〃	overmasters	〃	o'ermasters.
〃 52,	〃 2,	〃	reckles	〃	reckless.
〃 56,	〃 3,	〃	beids	〃	beeds.
〃 91,	〃 5 from bottom,	〃	Of	〃	Oh.

DRAMATIS PERSONÆ:

Sempronius.
Marcus Sempronius.
Cornelius Victor.
Theotimus.
Flaminius the Prefect.
The Flamen of Jupiter.
Flamens, Lictors, Centurions, Soldiers, Slaves etc.

Women:

Marcia.
Egeria.
Julia.

The Scene is at Rome during the persecution of the Christians in the reign of Dioclesian, A. D. 303.

ACT THE FIRST.

SCENE I.

A Hall in the Villa of Sempronius.

Enter SEMPRONIUS, MARCUS SEMPRONIUS, CORNELIUS VICTOR and MARCIA.

Sempronius.

To-morrow is the day the auspicious day
That joins our houses in a bond of love.
Cornelius Victor to thy arms I give
The fairest daughter of the noblest race.
Thy laurels with the myrtle must be twined,
And thou dost merit her: — be thine the charge
To dry the tears that fill her drooping eyes.
A maiden timid and retired as she
Leaves shrinkingly her childhood's haunts and joys;
And parting from her parents well may dim
The erst unclouded lustre of her brow.

Marcia.

Another cause conspires to grieve our child.
You know our city is infected quite
With that most deadly superstition,
Hateful to Gods and men. Theotimus, he,
The subtle Greek I speak of, who dwelt long
With Julius, an instructor of his son,
Suspected as a follower of this sect,
Has thence absconded, — is an outlaw now.

Egeria often met him — well you know
Her studious turn — and on his lips she hung
Curious to learn the wisdom that he taught.
Our noble kinsman too suspected lives,
Poor Julius! our Egeria loved him much.

Sempronius.

What madness can inspire such men to seek
A superstitious faith from Syria brought.
That these seditious tenets should be spread
Among the base Judean tribe is well.
But here at Rome, so favored by the Gods
Who led our legions, and our Senate ruled,
— 'Tis marvellous! and shews an evil time.
Swayed by the native Deities of Rome
Our conquering Eagles flew from shore to shore.
And now, when Dioclesian reigns supreme,
The Gods of Romulus, upon whose shrines
Rome Mistress of the world her offerings laid,
Are all deserted for a Godless Heaven.

Marcus Sempronius.

There's something in this baneful sect I loathe,
So dark and mystical! — how different far
From our gay smiling creed that sheds a charm
On every object both of sense and art.
E'en round the funeral urn are Roses twined;
And those who follow love and mirth and joy
Are votaries of the Gods our sires adored.

Enter Julia and Egeria.

But here fair Julia and Egeria come,
Their arms entwined, together gliding on:
One like the blushing Rose the Garden's Queen
All fresh, and fragrant opening to the Sun:

Egeria like the graceful Lily bends,
As lovely tho' less brilliant to the eye.

Cornelius.

Egeria, fairest, noblest of thy sex!
Behold our friends assembled all to view
The promise of thy hand and virgin troth.
But if reluctant thou art summoned here,
Think not that by compulsion I would gain
Thy beauty, altho' dearer than my life.
Tears dim thine eyes: ah! why, at such a time
When gay rejoicings fill thy natal halls
And all the household Gods look smiling on,
Should'st thou alone thus pale and pensive droop
Thy graceful head, and with averted looks
See thy once loved Cornelius sorrowing stand?
Egeria, is this kind to scorn me so?

Egeria.

Alas my Lord, think not my heart is false
To all its early vows, — my parent's choice.
I am unhappy — Ah! forgive these words —
But still am honoured by thy proffered hand.
Most noble youth, too well, too fondly loved:
— But this is not a time to speak such things.

Sempronius.

There is a solemn mystery in her words:
This comes of dealing in philosophy.
I grieve she ever met yon gloomy Greek:
Her's is the age of smiles and radiant joy.
Cornelius Victor this will pass away.
All is propitious; — she shall be thy bride:
And may the Gods upon your union shine.
To night in banquetting, and songs we'll join,
And roseate wreaths shall crown the flowing cups.

To-morrow, white robed Damsels move along
To chaunt the Hymenæan:
The nuptial torches lead the dancing train:
Playthings and Nuts are scattered to the throng;
And, in her saffron-coloured veil, behold
My own Egeria as thine honoured bride!

Slaves bring in dishes of Gold, vases of flowers and urns of perfume — then enter a group of Maidens and Youths who dance and scatter roses at the feet of the Guests.

Marcia.

Oh let me see one smile upon thy face:
Rejoice thy Father with a shew of joy.
Is he some tyrant to compel thy choice?
If not, why torture him with seeming grief?

Cornelius.

What has thus changed thee from thy former self?
Ah mornful change for beauty and for youth!
My loveliest own Egeria why so sad?

Egeria.

Oh! mock me not with flattering words my Lord.
I trust I am beloved; I love as well;
But know I am not fairer than the rest.

Cornelius.

It is not flattery when I call thee fair
And deem thee still the loveliest of thy sex.
There is a magic in thine every word:
Thy beauty never palls upon the sight.
What matters it what robe I see thee wear?
Pale be thy face, unjewelled be thy brow,
Egeria still is there: — it is not hues
Or features we adore: — Oh 'tis thyself!

Sempronius.

Thou wayward Girl! I can no more contain.

Canst thou so calmly listen to his praise
Who honours thee in choosing thee his bride?
This is caprice my son — We know the sex.
From 'neath those drooping lids no doubt she views
Thy noble presence with a secret joy.

Egeria.

I have no vain caprice: he knows me well.
Cornelius Victor take my hand, and heart.
My father, deal not harshly with thy child.
Alas! she loves too tenderly, too well.

Sempronius.

To-morrow then shall see our houses joined;
And Hymen, crowned with blooming flowers, shall fling
Clear flames of wedded love from out his torch.
Before the Lares incense shall be burnt;
And all the Gods propitiously look on
To celebrate the day that makes her thine.
Most noble Victor, when I give her thee
I do not blush; for she will not disgrace
Thine ancient name, tho' of the weaker sex.
Cornelia gave the virtuous Gracchi birth;
And, albeit courted by a monarch, chose,
A Roman citizen to be her Lord.
Portia was Cato's daughter, and she died,
A Roman Patriot's wife, a Roman's death.

Exeunt Sempronius, Marcia, Julia and Egeria.

Marcus Sempronius.

Why dost thou linger here, and pensive stand
With folded arms, and looks that woo the ground?
Has yon capricious girl the power to quell
Thy noble bearing, and to cloud that brow
Where valour proudly sat as on a throne?
Rouse thyself brave Cornelius, thou wilt lose

Thy lovely bride by humouring her caprice.
Follow her, woo her as a soldier ought
Who lays his well-won laurels at her feet.

Cornelius.

Thy kindness pains me: thou hast been to me
A second Father; and the Gods alone,
Who read the deep recesses of my heart,
Know that I willingly would shed my blood
To prove my gratitude for all thy care.
But blame me not if thus I love, and fear.

Marcus Sempronius.

I am repaid by seeing thee the first,
The best and noblest of our Roman Youth:
And, altho' young in years, renowned in arms:
The glory of our Legions, and thy race.
Thou wert a worthy son of ancient Rome
When not degenerate as we see her now.
To save my life, didst thou not risk thine own?
Thy buckler warded off the deadly blows
The foes of Rome and Dioclesian dealt.
That debt of gratitude my niece shall pay.

Cornelius.

Worthy Sempronius, to my youthful ears
How grateful sounds the praise of one like thee.
Austere thine aspect, that has power to quell
The eager petulance of forward youth.
But still for those whose earnest souls seek honour
Thy stirring words and deeds are trumpet-calls.
My prize was fair Egeria: she my crown:
And now — with scorn she views me at her feet.

Marcus Sempronius.

She loves thee Victor, canst thou doubt my words?
But she, unlike the beauties of our time,

The gay luxurious dames that court the gaze
Of each voluptuous, fond and forward youth;
In virgin modesty, and proud reserve
Hides her unrivalled charms from every eye.
She is more fitted for a Roman's bride.
Her beauty will not be a common shew.
Thy union blest with brave, and manly sons,
And daughters dowered with all their Mother's grace,
Honoured by men, and favoured by the Gods,
Will be the boast, and glory of thy name.

Cornelius.

Can it be weakness — this fond craving love
Which now I feel for her my promised bride?
For next my Country, next my native Rome,
Dear is Egeria to my yearning soul.
Oh! may the Gods propitiously incline
To bless our union, and to join our fates.

Marcus Sempronius.

Go brave Cornelius, seek my gentle niece.
Happy the hour! when I shall see her thine,
And thee a member of our noble house.
The bravest son of Rome may surely claim
The fairest of Rome's daughters for his bride.

Exeunt Marcus Sempronius, and Victor Cornelius.

SCENE II.

A Garden.

Enter Julia and Egeria.

Julia.

Here will we sit, and the last moments live
Of our twin life; while, all unmarked, the throng
Wakes the high hall to revelry within.

And as I kiss thee Sister tell me why,
I feel so gay and merry, when ere long
I shall be parted from thy gentle side —
Nay weep and laugh at once! altho' 'tis strange.
I weep to think that we must part so soon;
And tho' all smiles upon thy future path,
Yet how uncertain is a woman's fate:
How many anxious hopes, and fears divide
A sister's heart who loves so well as I!
Still I must laugh to think of thee a bride,
A Roman matron thou, and yet a child.

Egeria.

Sweet Julia, gentle Sister, far too well
I know thou lovest me — oh! love me less.
Think of thyself, thy fortunes; thou art young,
And youth has yet no bitterness for thee.
Be gay, be happy, and our parents joy.
Oh! would I could repay their tender care,
Best, fondest parents of a hapless child!
Oh Julia! kindest, truest, gentlest friend,
Pity thy poor Egeria, weep with her.

Julia.

Yes I will weep, for — quite unlike thyself,
Now seldom does a smile adorn thy cheek:
And yet thou wedst with one thine early choice,
Noble and brave, whom glory names her own.
His budding laurels lie before thy feet.
But thou art changed, since first thou cam'st to know
Yon gloomy Greek.
One of that baneful and detested sect,
Blasphemers of our Gods, and sacred rites.

Egeria.

Thou know'st them not my Julia: — say no more.

These men thou deem'st blasphemers, in thine anger,
Pure are their lives and holy is their creed.
That creed — no idle dream of sinful men —
Gives Truth and Hope, to point the way to Heaven.
— But thou art ignorant — wherefore should I chide?

Julia.

Surely thou canst not plead an Atheist's cause?
But let us leave its votaries to their fate:
They meet the death so richly they deserve.
To morrow sees these superstitious men
Within the Arena brought, and there they pay
Due offerings to the Gods, or else they die.

Egeria.

Speak not exultingly of crimes like these.
The hour may come thou wilt repent thy rage,
And wish one victim of the herd was saved;
And that thy tongue had spared the general blame:
— Unsay the injurious words, — if thou dost love me.

Julia.

Ah! do I love thee? I have loved too well:
A love surpassing far a Sister's love.
When near to thee, I had no other thought
But to live in thee: — I did prize myself
Because I was thy sister: thus I shone
By a reflected light.
Cornelius cannot love thee more than I.
But little dost thou heed his love, or mine:
Yon gloomy Greek is dearer to thy heart.

Egeria.

Yet there is something that might make thee change
Despite of all thy tenderness and truth.
Let but the High Priest with his train appear
To claim me as a Christian for his prey:

Julia.

Here would I hold thee and turn back their arms.
But still thou art not such! it cannot be.
Where couldst thou ever learn this hateful creed?
Think of our mother, of Cornelius think.
Alas! I tremble lest my fears prove true.

Egeria.

Oh! my dear Sister, now the hour is come
To prove thy love; I can no more disguise
The awful truth, it must be told at last.
Thinkst thou that willingly I 'd give thee pain?
But wouldst thou have me worship Gods that once
Our evil passions did create on earth?
Alas! what mean these tears? these rising sobs.

Julia.

Ah me! ah me! all ruined, all undone:
Egeria, this is madness, or a dream.
Thou art deluded, do not speak our shame:
At least conceal it for our mother's sake.
Behold I kneel, spare her, spare me, thyself;
And poor Cornelius, him who loves thee so.
Oh! that I ever should behold this hour.
Thou an apostate! — oh! away, away.

Egeria.

Reproach me not dear sister. 'tis enough
That I have lost the world, and all I prize:
That I am most unhappy. 'tis enough
To see thy grief: oh! do not add thy hate.
Forgive just heaven! these tears to weakness due.
A little month ago, and I was gay
— But now how changed, alas! how sadly changed!

Julia.

Yes thou art changed indeed: I know thee not:

For I remember thee the merriest child,
More lively than myself, and now, thine eyes
Are bent on earth: I see thee silent stand
With drooping arms: in vain I try each art —
The lute, the dance, — to bring a smile again
Upon thy pensive cheek! ah, cruel girl!
Thou wilt not smile to make thy Julia glad.

Egeria.

Ah! do not think of me: I was not born
For love, or happiness; but think of those
Who merit all thy tenderness, and smiles.

Julia.

I cannot joy when thus I see thee sad:
It is unnatural: on my breast recline,
And tell me all thy secret griefs, and pains.
Say thou wert dreaming; and forget the past.
Thy words were surely ravings of the brain.

Egeria.

I hear the hooting of the solemn owl:
Within the cypress tree he nightly sits.
The twitter of the birds among the boughs
Feebler and feebler, marks the close of day.
A thousand clouds are travelling o'er the skies,
Chasing each other thro' the viewless air.
There is a tempest brooding in the Heavens:
Such an oppression on my brow I feel.

Julia.

Thy mind is fevered: — rather 'tis a night
For lovers to hold converse with the moon.
Here is Cornelius, may his words avail
To bring thee back thyself and happiness.

Exit JULIA.

Enter Cornelius.

Egeria, sweet Egeria, is it thou
I find here thus alone! Oh blessed chance!
Here let me stay, my beautiful, mine own.

Egeria.

Yes, it is he! — Ah fatal, dreaded hour!
Alas Cornelius! is it me thou seek'st?
Tell all thy wishes: speak thy soul's desire.

Cornelius.

Look my beloved, what a night is this:
How bright yon moon is shining from above,
Bathing the clouds in her immortal light.
The streams, upleaping from their marble founts,
Scatter cool pearl-spray on the sultry air.
Egeria let thy gentle accents breathe
Like soothing music on my listening ear:
Speak fairer Goddess of so fair a heaven.

Egeria.

It is a mournful night. Cornelius say
Dost thou remember when in childish hours
We chased each other on this terrace walk,
And thou wouldst gather every simple flower
To deck my hair, dost thou remember this?
A thousand memories on each memory wait.
Oh! we were merry children, could we live
For ever children, always young, and gay!
Oh! why are guilt, and sorrow in the world?
Why not for ever young, for ever gay?

Cornelius.

My own Egeria! why so sad to-night?
Art thou not young, and gay, and mine alone:
Then why recall the past? why fall these tears?

Like gems that tremble on the blushing rose.
Dropt from the eyelids of the amorous morn?

Egeria.

Cornelius, dear Cornelius: let me rest
My head upon thy shoulder: I am faint.
The evening breeze has chilled my inmost heart.
To-morrow — ah! who knows? another sun
Will never see us here: oh! never more.

CORNELIUS gives her the Passion Flower.

Cornelius.

Look here Egeria, look upon my gift.
Thou badst me seek for thee this simple flower;
And here it is, — nay why these sudden tears!

Egeria.

That flower! and from thy hands! a simple flower!
— Restores my soul to virtue, and to Heaven.
Oh sacred gift! here rest upon my heart,
So weak, irresolute, and yet so true.

Cornelius.

Give me one smile, since thus my gift is prized.
Thou seest that absent, still I think on thee.
My only love, my dear my gentle bride.

Egeria.

Call me no more that name, — or rather say
It o'er and o'er, sweet music to mine ear, —
The dying knell of dear departed days.
For oh! this is the last, last fatal time
I ever shall drink in those much-loved sounds.
One little word dissolves the dream of joy:
'T were better spoken, and then all is o'er.
Cornelius dost thou love me?

Cornelius.

Love thee!

Thou know'st it is a mockery to ask.
But what wouldst thou reveal, what fatal tale?

Egeria.

Nay do not shrink nor shudder, — say again
I love thee dear Egeria as myself.

Cornelius.

Thou canst not doubt the fondness of my love,
Distract me not then with thy dubious words.

Egeria.

And shall we meet no more? oh lost to me,
Ere I reveal the fatal, dreaded truth.
Stay not so near me, leave me, leave me here,
More distant, still more distant ere I speak.

Cornelius.

Egeria, by our former faithful love,
By all the hopes of happiness we prized,
The mutual tenderness of plighted vows,
Speak to me, tell me if I merit this.

Egeria.

Alas! a fearful gulf hath yawned between us:
Dare not to pass it, or I lose my soul.
Leave me, desert me, never see me more:
Farewell Cornelius, noblest, dearest, best:
I am a Christian, lost to love and thee.

EGERIA alone. Enter FLAMINIUS the Prefect, followed by a Slave.

Flaminius to his Slave.

Remain without, until I bid thee hither. Exit Slave.

Flaminius.

Alone, and weeping on thy bridal eve!
What mean these tears? why wouldst thou glide away?
Say dost thou shun me, or from hate, or fear,
And cast thy tearful eyes upon the ground

Lest I should read some secret meaning there?
But leave me not: strange rumours are abroad
To thy discredit: I must speak — attend.
Upon my will depends thy life or death.
For this I sought thee secret and alone.

Egeria.

I know thee well Flaminius, far too well
And that thou wouldst my ruin and my death.
I know thee well. alas! there was a time
When by thy flatteries, and thine impious arts
Thou mightst have gained an empire o'er my soul;
And I have fallen in the deadly toils
That superstition for her victims weaves.
But now mine eyes are opened; — he I love
Is one thou hatest: yet thou must respect
The Deity I serve.

Flaminius.

— A Jewish God!
Young maiden say no more; thy steps are watched:
Thy looks, thy thoughts are read; too truly read:
Hate me, despise me, — thou art in my power.
Egeria listen, I may save thee yet.
Thou art a Christian, and thou knowst the fate
That dogs the votaries of this creed proscribed.
As yet no human tongue can prove thy guilt.
Thou shalt not die: — go, gaze upon that form,
That beauteous form, those dark love-beaming eyes:
Go, and desert thy cold, and gloomy sect.
Give thyself to our laughter-loving Gods
Tread on the cross, Egeria and be mine.

Egeria.

Avaunt thou ruthless man, I scorn thy love:
Thy love, and cruel threats I scorn alike.

I am the bride of one whose very look
Would make thee tremble if I called him hither
To avenge this insult: — hence thou impious man
Exert thy utmost power: revenge my scorn:
For I defy thy hate, and spurn thy love.

Exit Egeria.

Flaminius.

Defy my hate, and spurn my love! 'Tis well.
Thou shalt repent. My love is changed to hate.
Yes! go thou scornful maiden, go, and seek
Thy favoured lover: go, and mock my love.
But thou art in my toils: perchance ere long
I shall behold that stubborn pride give way;
And see thee, at my feet, renounce thy Gods.
Egeria mine! — I dare not hope such bliss;
But if not mine she never shall be his.

Enter Slave.

Come hither Slave: here, take this purse of gold.
Thou knowst how baneful is this Christian sect
That now so widely spreads despite our laws.
Its followers are accused of every crime
That shuns the light of day. A cruel death
Awaits them all: the Emperor wills it so.
Much I suspect the daughter of this house
Is tainted with that plague-spot; much I fear
She will not serve before our ancient shrines;
But joins in the assemblies of these zealots,
To meet their Priests and celebrate their rites.

Slave.

My Lord, by thy desire, for many days
I've watched the Lady when she heeded not
That I was by; and at the midnight hour
Twice has she left her home and sought alone

The cypress grove where all her fathers sleep.
At first I deemed she met Cornelius there
Her destined Lord; but, by the glimmering light
Of the pale moon, I saw an aged man
Clad as a Greek, no lover, by her side.

Flaminius.

Egeria thou art mine. there is no way
Thou canst escape. Slave thou hast done my bidding.
I long surmised her falsehood, watch her well.
Thou knowst thy duty; do not quit this house;
But hover near until the evening hour:
Let who will leave it, be they strictly watched;
And where the young Egeria bends her steps
Follow her closely if she goes alone.
Hast thou her safe entrapped? Hie thee to me:
— Another heavy purse of gold is thine.

Slave.

Here will I watch until to-morrow's sun;
And then my Lord the purse of gold is mine:
The Lady kneels before our sared shrines;
Abjures her creed, and gives herself to thee;
Or amid frightful tortures she shall feel
Thy hate is not a mockery: — he she loves
The doating youth who holds her to be his
Will it delight him still to call her so,
When he shall view that face all stained with tears,
The lustre of those eyes with terror dimmed,
Pallid the lips that breathed the vows of love,
And cold the hand he warmly clasped in his?
No! he will leave her, leave her to her shame:
And then the Christian maiden will be thine.

Flaminius.

Yes, this shall be my hent: but will she bend

Her haughty soul to sue for mercy then,
Deserted by her lover and her God?
  Ye Deities who rule the fate of men,
The hour that sees her dying at my feet
Will be your triumph, when I bring at last
The victim due to your neglected shrines.

Exeunt.

END OF ACT THE FIRST.

ACT THE SECOND.

SCENE I.

Outside a sepulchral vault.

Enter EGERIA.

Egeria.

The moon burns dim in yon black cypress' top:
A drear sepulchral lamp. How many hearts
Are mouldering in this dust that once throbbed quick,
As mine throbs now, with anxious hopes and fears.
The forms of revelry that chased me hither
Vanish before these solemn images.
— For joyous kindred, pale ancestral statues:
For gairish torchlight, deep funereal gloom:
For ringing cymbals, the stern calm of death.
Ah me! I feel the night-damps on my brow:
Descending heavily they chill my heart.
The stars are shrouded in the gathering wrack:
The midnight wind is moaning through the pines.
How grim the sky! Just Heaven! Is it thy will
That one so all-untutored as myself
Should be thus sorely tried? — I am too young.

Enter THEOTIMUS.

Theotimus.

How pale thy cheek my child — tears in thine eye.
What direful fears invade thy gentle breast?
What fresh alarms? say wouldst thou now retract?

Egeria.

My father let me bend my knee to thee
And kiss thy guiding hand. Oh! let my grief
Be here poured forth; and do not chide thy child
That she is weak: look on my tender youth
In luxury reared, a stranger to all grief.
But think not I retract, or shrink from pain.
Bring me before the scaffold, I am firm.
Let Lions loose to tear these tender limbs;
And Romans shall admire a Roman death.
But — say is it a crime? it cannot be —
I love Cornelius, my affianced Lord.
To morrow is the day should seal our vows.
And I have said — oh father! I have said
The word that has condemned me in his sight.
I cannot bear his hate, outlive his scorn.

Theotimus.

The hate of Heaven is yet more hard to bear.
And is the hour arrived that I must see
Christ's handmaid, once again a slave to man;
Forswearing for his love her faith, her hope?
Go! Seek thy heathen Gods, and worship them.

Chorus of Christian converts within the Tower.

Egeria.

Oh! let me join that heaven-revealing chaunt.
Father behold thy child: — reject me not.
These tears that flow so bitterly, so fast
Attest my contrite heart, my steady will.

Theotimus.

Lady come on, and join the holy choir.
A weak old man conducts the airy steps
Of her the fairest, noblest of her race,
Who leaves her festive halls, and silken couch

To seek these gloomy crypts, these secret rites,
To worship here the true, the only God.

THEOTIMUS and EGERIA ascend the steps and descend into the Vault.

SCENE II.

Within the sepulchral Tower. Aged and young Men and Girls christian converts.

Enter THEOTIMUS and EGERIA.

Theotimus.

Beloved followers of a creed proscribed,
Who here assemble in this vault of death
To celebrate our pure and holy rites,
Behold another convert to our faith
Of high degree, reared in luxurious ease.
She quits her purple couch, her perfumed halls,
She comes to join a persecuted sect;
And slights all earth can give, to win the skies.

Egeria.

And am I midst the followers of your creed
The men whom calumny has still pursued
And taxed with every crime? Oh! would your foes
Could witness here your rites, and see your deeds.
Innocuous all their evil words must fall
On such as you my father, such as these
Pure virtuous maidens whom I joy to embrace.

Theotimus.

This is our superstition: — would indeed
Our enemies but once could see aright
These guileless creatures in pure union bound.
Ours are no artful dreams of lying men,

No blood-stained Deities, no impious rites;
But Heaven, and virtue, are our hope, and guide.
And yet my children when I see around
These youths so brave, so goodly in their strength,
And these sweet maidens in their hour of prime,
Tears fill mine aged eyes: it matters not
How soon my feeble limbs are laid in dust,
But you — so young, so innocent, so fair! —
Nay let not earthborn fears untune our souls
For His most holy Service: rather find we
In Prayer and Praise a more than conquering strength.

HYMN.

Father! Be thy Name adored,
Sped o'er earth thy conquering Word,
On all hearts thy Spirit poured.

Give us of that strengthening bread
Which our Elder Brother fed: —
Daily portions of thy Will
Such as we too may fulfil.
Till our heavenward glance be bright
And our spirit full of light.

Stay our souls with draughts of love
From the quickening fount above: —
Twice-blest mercy, still receiving
Pardon freely, freely giving.
Raised at length in that embrace
Grant us to behold thy face.

Father! If it be thy Will,
Keep thy Church from earthly ill.

Save us from the Lion's fang;
Save us from the Torturer's pang:
From the Lictor's rod of shame,
From the robe of smouldering flame:
From what worse there yet may be
Left of Christ's great agony.

Yet again we pray thee Father,
Hear and save — Oh save us rather
From the evil we inherit,
Sinfulness of heart and spirit:
From the coward fear of pain,
From the lust for pleasures vain,
From the greed of worldly gain.

Thou, even here, canst give us peace:
Thou canst give us swift release:
— Caught to Christ: — might we aspire
To the Martyr's throne of fire,
Like Elijah's car ascending,
While the Conqueror downward bending
O'er his brethren from above
Casts the mantle of his love.

Father, bless our friendly foes:
Feel we not, through these, the throes
Of our martyr-birth to Glory?
Know we not that deathless story
Shall preserve this seed of life
Through thy Church's after-strife;
Till the Persecutor's heart
Kindling choose the Sufferer's part:
Till Earth's countless tribes be one
In thy Spirit, through thy Son.

Egeria.

Break off — Break off! What fearful sounds are these?
We are betrayed! Again — I hear the steps
Of our pursuers: whither can we fly?
There is no help: kind Heaven! assist me now.
I see their lance-points, see their torches blaze:
I hear the clashing of their cruel arms.
Look up: Alas! I am not fit to die.

Theotimus.

Kneel, kneel my children round me, let them come,
Take me alone, and spare my guiltless lambs.
Whilst here I stay secure, and trust in God.
He will not leave his servants in their need.

Soldiers descend with blazing torches.

Centurion.

Here are the miscreants: seize, arrest them all.
Deliver up your weapons, or ye die.
Search all the vault, if any be concealed.
Ye impious men, it well befits your sect
Here in this darkness to perform your rites.
Degenerate! Faithless to your native Gods!
Traitors to Cæsar! Traitors to great Rome!
And you unhappy maidens here seduced,
The victims of these base, fanatic Jews,
And blent with sorcerers in unhallowed rites,
Let not the light discover who ye are;
But veil your faces, and conceal your shame.

JULIA descends the steps.

Julia.

The slave who has betrayed them told me true:
There is my sister; let me come to her.
Oh! spare her, spare the innocent, the young:

Unfetter her, release her, on my knees
I beg for mercy. Here is gold, take all!
She is betrayed, belied, — Hold off your hands:
Ye shall not touch her: — oh! away, away.

Egeria.

Heaven give me strength to bear this hour of trial
For I am faint with watching, and with grief.
Leave me, my generous Julia, leave me here.
Spare me thine anguish at this fatal hour
One farewell fond embrace, then let me go,
And trust in God, whatever doom befal.

Julia.

Here will I cling until they drag me hence,
My sweet, my innocent, mine own belov'd.
Oh save her, save her, unrelenting men!
And do not curse her: let me go with her.
Pity mine agony, my frenzied grief.
Men! Nay barbarians! See my tresses fall
Dishevelled on the pavement, see my tears.
A Roman maiden begs a Roman's life.

Theotimus.

Rise noble lady: leave thy sister here:
For He who guards his own will watch o'er her.

Julia.

Ha! is it thou! thou base deceiving man, —
Thy fatal arts misled the simple girl.
Seize him, the Atheist, seize the Christian Jew.

Egeria.

Julia I blush to see thee, thus distraught,
Assail this venerable, holy man.
For shame! it is not maidenly, nor fit.
Replace thy veil, compose thy scattered hair;
Seek out my sire, and tell him of my fate.

Sir, take this gentle maiden to thy charge;
Convey her to Sempronius: ah! she faints.
Poor girl she loved me much, one farewell kiss.

Centurion.

Confide in me: my service shall be paid
To this most noble lady now my charge.
My comrades come; our watch is nearly done:
Here with our christian prisoners let us mount.
To horse, to horse; away to reap the prize:
The Tribune waits, the Jailers ready stand.

Exeunt omnes.

SCENE III.

Outside the sepulchral Tower.

Enter the Prefect Flaminius followed by a Slave.

Flaminius.

Say didst thou see Egeria as she went?
Proudly she bore her: as she past the tree
Where we lay hid, the moon shone brightly forth:
I think she saw me, for she look'd so calm.
She could not choose but fear: but that deep pride
That never will desert her, gave her strength:
And I was trembling, but it was not terror:
I felt my brain on fire: — didst hear that sound?
'Tis thunder: hearken to Jove's awful voice.
It must portend disasters — hark! again.

Slave.

The sky lowers overhead: a storm is brooding.
Yet 'twas not thunder 'twas the howling wind
That rages in yon dark sepulchral vault.
But still the night is murky: warning drops
Fall heavily: let us begone in time.

Flaminius.

Didst thou not mark where fell yon thunderbolt?
The owl, ill-omened bird is shrieking nigh
All evil spirits surely are abroad.
Say sawst thou not yon aged prisoner pass,
Who followed poor Egeria? he was bound
In iron fetters, yet how calm his brow.
He dies to morrow, and his placid mien
Wore not one trace of terror, or of hate.
Speak, must I envy such as these? as these: —
Apostates, traitors, false to Heaven and Man?
And yet they smile at death, whilst I — fear death.
Danger I scorn, sharp torture I can bear.
It is the loss of life, of thought, I dread.
Let me feel misery, only let me feel:
But not to feel at all — to sleep for ever —
All, all this active being quench'd at once!
If not — to endure for aye what legends tell —
Oh! no I cannot, dare not, will not die.
I'd gladly be the vilest worm that crawls
The earth; the monster most abhor'd by man.
I cling to life as the poor drowning wretch
Clutches at straws to save himself from sinking.
— Yet she can die unmoved — what form is that?
It is my evil genius haunts my path?
Flaminius is deserted by his Gods.

Slave.

Come let us hence my Lord: I see no form,
The mists of night are rising from the earth,
And as they rise they take such various shapes
As our distempered fancy gives to them.
Let us away: the prisoners are secured:
Egeria, to her father's house conveyed,

Will there remain until the trial hour.
The facts are powerful to prove her guilt;
And she must die the death she does not fear.

Flaminius.

Yes she shall die, I see it must be so;
And let me cast these coward fears away.
This gloomy spot, and these ill-omened sounds
Had quite unmanned me: now I am myself.
I would have pitied her, have spared her life:
But it is vain, I saw that fearless brow,
That placid look she wore in passing hence.
Her doom is fixed; I know she will not yield;
And the infernal Gods demand their prey.

Exeunt FLAMINIUS and the Slave.

SCENE IV.

A Hall in Sempronius' Villa.

Enter SEMPRONIUS followed by a Slave, then CORNELIUS.

Sempronius.

What is this news ye tell me? 'tis a dream;
And ye deceive me. I, a Roman Chief
Renowned in arms, and in the senate first;
And now my child arrested in a vault,
Confederate with a base ignoble band.
It cannot be: — slaves ye shall die for this.
Ye glorious Gods my ancestors revered
Will ye thus view my shame with tranquil eyes,
Nor hurl your thunderbolts upon your foes,
Who have seduced my child, my once loved child?
Have I not paid due incense at your shrines,
And daily offerings on your altars laid?

And am I now deserted in my need?
Perish the slave who brings this fatal news.

Cornelius.

Refrain thy sudden hand mine honoured Lord
Remember what thou art: — 'tis surely false:
Or by some evil chance she wandered thither.
If it be true — alas! she is thy child:
And thou must save her from impending doom.

Sempronius.

Unduteous child, blasphemer of our Gods!
— No rather curse her — she shall die the death.
And yet she is my child: it seems to me
But yesterday I held her on my knee
A little prattling thing, an april bud,
Light of mine eyes, and treasure of my heart.
She was so beautiful, her mother's pride.
My child, my child — oh! this is weak indeed,
A Roman — still a Father —
Where is my Daughter? let the worst be known.

Cornelius.

By some untoward chance, or magic art
The wily Greek, Theotimus, has escaped:
The other christian converts are secured
And now in different prisons, but thy child —
In deference to thy name, she is allowed
Here to remain until the hour of trial:
To morrow Dioclesian has ordained
That those accused as followers of this faith
Shall in the Arena be brought forth and tried;
There to deny their Gods and bend the knee
Before the altars of immortal Jove
Or else they die. I dare not even think
Upon their fearful death: wild beasts let forth

Half famished; roaring fiercely for their prey!
Egeria summoned thither! Grant it heaven
Her Mother's fond entreaties may avail
To change her purpose and avert her fate.

Sempronius.

The Gods provoked by her have left my house;
And well her blasphemy deserves their hate.
Oh! Jove, great Jove, the King of Gods and Men,
Wilt thou allow thy altars to be scorned
By these fanatic Jews? Eternal Rome
The great, the free, polluted by this sect,
This pestilence of error, sees her best
Her noblest children by such madness lost.
Thy temples thus deserted for a creed
Alecto from the infernal regions brought
To spread disunion, and to poison life.
— Take from the pillars those sweet hanging wreaths,
Build, build the funeral pile, and light the torch.
Rent be your garments, veiled be every head,
For I have lost my daughter, she is dead.

Cornelius.

My honoured father! by that cherished name
I still must call thee tho' it is a name
Now fatal to thine ears: oh! check thy grief.
Let us devise some means to save my bride
For even guilty I will deem her such.
The Emperor is severe, he hates this sect:
But surely our entreaties may prevail,
May lead her — if no more — to hide her shame,
And spare her fallen father this disgrace.

Sempronius.

Yes I am fallen indeed from what I was.
Once did I glory in the Roman name:

But oh! the Gods have left me in my age;
And I must humbly bend, and veil my head.
Why did the Powers presiding o'er my fate
Give me a son to take him back again?
My boy! my boy! he was a noble child.
He might have lived, ye unrelenting Heavens
Had ye so willed, and I a Roman Sire.
And now where is my boy? cold, lifeless clay.
My daughter lives but to disgrace my name.
Rise, rise ye Furies from your dread abodes,
Infernal Deities arise, with all
Your snakes and torches! Pity me great Jove:
Pity thy worshipper, and spare my house.
Adieu Cornelius! I must hence to seek
The augurs: — and now let their omens shew
If the Sempronii are condemned to fall,
Or offerings may appease the offended Gods.

Exit Sempronius.

Enter a Slave.

Slave.

An aged man a stranger by his dress
Demands admittance and would see my Lord.

Cornelius.

Admit him quick, perhaps it is some friend
Of poor Egeria who would save her life.

Enter Theotimus disguised.

Cornelius.

Who art thou stranger, and what wouldst thou here?

Theotimus.

Theotimus is my name, my country Greece;
A Greek my sire, my mother was a Jew.
I am a Christian, and I crave admission
To one who is a follower of that way.

Cornelius.

Accurst and shameless! Comest thou to this house
To mock the ills thy magic here hath wrought?
I harm thee not: but, wouldst thou save thy life,
Begone, and brave not her stern father's ire.

Theotimus.

Say, art thou he Egeria was to wed,
Her Lord affianced, known for noble deeds?

Cornelius.

I am Cornelius: my betrothed bride
Thy sorceries have slain: what wouldst thou more?

Theotimus.

Most noble Sir, despite thy scornful glance,
Thy haughty bearing and thy wounding words,
There is a spirit throned upon that brow
Leads me to endure in silence thy reproach,
Nay count thee worthy of the Christian name.

Cornelius.

Dream not old man. I was not born to crouch
A craven bondsman 'neath an alien law.
Humility that grovels in the dust
But ill beseems a son of conquering Rome.
Where are the victories by your warriors won?
Where are the states your sages have built up?
— The stern devotion to their country's cause:
The selfless daring in her just defence: —
Where are the Fabii, Scipios, Catos found
Among your votaries: — where a Roman heart?

Theotimus.

Come to the Arena when to-morrow's sun
Shall gild yon pompous temples with its light
To view these grovelling bondsmen from the stake
Fling smiling back again your proffered grace.

Boast of your sages fortitude, and vaunt
Your patriots dying for their country's cause —
All an admiring world to view their fall:
Then see these poor, despised, unfriended men,
Outlawed, deserted by their nearest kin,
See them exposed to torture, and contempt,
Look up to Heaven, and calmly wait their death.

Cornelius.

'Tis true: ye have a courage e'en in guilt.
I know thy creed: in happier days I heard
Poor Julius on that theme discourse in vain.
Thy gloomy zeal bids timid maidens rave.
Renouncing every social, sacred tie,
They headlong rush to death by sorcerers led.
It is a madness, not true stoic pride,
That bids thy votaries fearless court their doom.

Theotimus.

There is no pride I grant thee in our creed,
Our lowly Master taught humility.
Poor fragile mortals of the passing hour,
Creatures of clay, in sin and sorrow born,
What pride befits the bosom of such beings?
Or if we have a pride it bids us bear
The world's contempt, the bitterness of death:
The pride of truth, of virtue, of ourselves
Now made immortal by the words of life.

Cornelius.

Old man I pity thee, for in thy words
I do discern a spirit might beseem
A Roman warrior, and I must lament
To see thy zeal and eloquence perverted
By an enslaving superstition.

Thus much I owe thee; and now, part in safety:
Return not, as thou tenderest thy life.

Theotimus.

Then Heaven forgive thee, for I came to bring
The words of hope and comfort to thy bride.
The day may come thou wilt repent this hour.

Cornelius.

Stay, if thou com'st to join thy voice with ours,
Egeria may be conquered by thy words
And we shall owe her precious life to thee.

Theotimus.

Thou dost mistake, the words of hope I bring,
Are not the words that thou wouldst wish to hear,
My hope is of another, better world,
Beyond this idle transitory life.
My comfort fain would strengthen her to bear
All things in suffering for her holy faith.

Cornelius.

Begone cold heartless Jew, and bless her name
Whom thou didst seek, I have not seized on thee,
Base renegade from thine own country's Gods.
Canst thou then see, by thy infernal arts
The young, the beautiful condemn'd to die
And hug in safety thy mean worthless life?

Theotimus.

Oh! would to Heaven that I alone might die
To save my children, would to Heaven I might
Be taken from this world of sin and woe.
But I have still my task, nor dare I raise,
Through weariness or cowardice, my hand
Against my proper life, as Cato dared.
But when my hour arrives, come thou and see
A Christian fearless as a Roman die.

END OF ACT THE SECOND.

ACT THE THIRD.

SCENE I.

A garden in Sempronius' villa.

Enter EGERIA.

My couch is sleepless, my repose unrest.
I will behold again the rising sun,
Breathe my last breath in fresh and fragrant air,
And bless once more yon purpling Alban hills.
Ah! when I lift my wondering glance and see
Heavens golden cloud-thrones pierced with arrowy light
And moon and stars pale in the lustrous shower,
My senses are entranced: methinks there quires
Sweet music from yon spheres, filling their course
With harmony divine; and now the clouds
Like Prophets throned and splendour-robéd saints
Bend in devotion round the shrine of day.
The spicy herbs I tread beneath my feet,
By that oppression made more odorous,
The orange buds that fall upon my breast
And the fair rose that opes its balmy leaves
To bathe its blossoms in the tears of night
All breathe their incense to the Lord of all.
See herald Morn gives place to jocund Day
Flushing with regal triumph, hailed with joy
By all: — by all but one. A wretch forlorn,
Disowned and cast aside, I bid farewell
To this enchanting world: — enchanting world

Farewell: — and feel I not my spirit bathed
In founts of hidden strength to break thy charm?
Knowing thee better I had loved thee less,
And scarce had felt a pang to leave thee now.
Merciful Heaven! Forgive these last regrets
And, though through suffering, take me to thyself.

Enter MARCIA and CORNELIUS.

Marcia.

Here is the ungrateful child, cause of our woe,
This night she hath not lain upon her couch,
But wandered forth a stranger to all rest.
Thy father sends us — do not steel thy heart
To his entreaties, listen to our prayers.
I do conjure thee, by a mother's anguish,
A father's lifelong care, a daughter's duty;
Oh rend not thou our hearts with grief and shame.
Cornelius comes too: — still would call thee his.
My Lord Cornelius I will leave you with her.
Oh! seek some art to win me back my daughter.
Let love's soft magic o'er your words preside,
Or I have lost my child, my son, my life.

Exit MARCIA.

Egeria.

Behold me here to wait this bold discourse
That must subdue my will, and move my heart:
And speak it freely, we are strangers now.
Thy once-loved voice is foreign to mine ear.
So reason well, persuasion skills no more.
The past is buried with my former faith.

Cornelius.

Egeria, is it thou I hear, and see,
My bride affianced and my promised love?
Oh no, it is thy semblance, not thyself!

Yet still that breathing loveliness is there,
That heavenly spirit in its beauteous shrine.
There are the flowing ringlets I have twined
In playful dalliance with a daring hand.
There are the rosy lips I sighed to press,
And there that hand so warm with life and hope
Where the blue rivulet veins visit at will
Their lilied faery realm — ah! mine no more.
Oh! yes it is Egeria, 'tis my bride.
Behôld Cornelius kneels to worship thee.
Renounce thy gloomy creed, and live for love.

Egeria.

Arise my Lord. I should be stern, and chide
Both thy presumption, and thy impious speech;
But that my woman's nature will have way,
And being weak myself I pardon thee.
Thy ignorance pleads excuses for thy guilt.
And ah! The memories of our early love,
— I dare not feign a virtue I possess not —
Have filled my heart with grief, mine eyes with tears:
A momentary softness — 'tis profane,
But all those tender images of love
Of former heathen fondness made my heart
Beat faster in this bosom; hateful throbs
Of passion knocking at its former home.
'Tis past, and doubtless this rebuke was due
To check the arrogance, and upstart pride
Of virtue newly gained, and proudly borne.
But my resolve is fixed, this very pang
At parting tells me that we needs must part.

Cornelius.

Alas! I know thee not, thou art estranged
From all thy former ties of birth and love.

Heartless and cold, alas! I know thee not.
And what has changed thee but thy hateful creed,
And torn thee from thy parents and thy home
And from thy lover? — I had been to thee
A guardian, husband, lover all in one.
Yet thou canst leave me, and without a tear.
Go then ungrateful, cruel, scornful girl.
I leave thee to thy fate — I can no more.
Nor look on thee again, lest I relent.

Egeria.

Stay yet Cornelius — we must part indeed,
But not in anger, do not leave me thus.
Tho' I seem harsh, thou canst not, wilt not know
How much this harshness costs me — stay awhile,
Let me conjure thee by our former love:
For in my heart thou dwell'st, and ever wilt.
Not as the object of mere earthly passion;
My love, far deeper now, would gain thy soul:
Thy soul, more precious than yon quickening orb,
Eternal, sacred, both to me, and Heaven.
Look to that Heaven through me: — a feeble girl,
Points out the only way that leads to life.
Worship'st thou me? Oh fond and impious thought
To worship thus the creature! — rather say
Thou worship'st self, and earthly love in me.

Cornelius.

Talk not of love — some wretch hath steeled thy heart
Against thy former fondness — 'Tis a crime
To love — the gentle ties of love are base.
Oh! hateful creed! detested, cruel Faith!
Has it not marred thy gentle nature quite
And made thee unrelenting, cold and harsh?
I loath thy creed, for it has reft from me

My sweet, mine own Egeria — she was once
All yielding softness, all frank loveliness,
And now —

Egeria.

Say on and now, what am I now?
I have no more 'tis true the female art
That sought to please, and rule, and knew the way.
I ruled by yielding, and with softness swayed;
I loved thee, I was lovely, that I knew;
And could we live for ever, it were well
In dreams of loveliness, and love to live.
But we must die; and ah! to die for ever —
Past are those hours that once I vainly deemed
Were fraught with happiness, and hope for me:
I blush to recollect those worldly joys.
Yes — that Egeria of blind-hearted passion
Is dead: another stands before thee now
And calls thee to new life and deathless love.

Cornelius.

Thou speak'st in riddles — mine no more — yet stay
Perverse and heartless, I abjure thee quite.
I leave thee to thy fate, and may thy Gods
Reward thee for the lover thou hast lost.

Exit Cornelius.

Egeria.

And art thou gone my earliest, latest love?
Ah couldst thou read this heart, this yearning heart,
Thou wouldst not then ungenerous deem her harsh
Who would recall thee dearest if she dared.
Forgive me Heaven this sigh, it is the last.
And now farewell to love, a long farewell:
And welcome death: life has no life for me.

I have lost all on earth: come therefore death
Come claim thy victim — there was once a time
I should have grieved to quit yon deep calm sky
And all this tranquil nature that contrasts
With the wild tumult of my heaving breast.
Alas! I love him — can it be a crime?
He was my destined husband, lover, friend.
Oh! let me pray for strength, for I am weak,
My reason and my feelings are at war.
To-morrow, doubtless, will my trial come.
I must be strong in Faith, and firm in Hope.
Come Faith, come Hope, and renovate my heart.
Assist me Heaven! without thy aid I fall.
Alas! I see my honoured uncle comes.

Enter Marcus Sempronius.

Marcus Sempronius.

Sent by thy noble parents I must join
My voice to theirs to move thy wayward will
Thy father, mother, sister weeping wait,
Their happiness depends upon thy words.

Egeria.

Dear uncle, do not urge my parent's love,
My sister's tenderness, — I know it all.
Their grief unnerves me, and I must be strong.
I have a work, a noble work to do.
Oh seek not my dishonour: let me die
At least respected by the men who slay me.

Marcus Sempronius.

Thou shalt not die — I will not let thee go —
What madness urges thee to seek a tomb?

Unhappy, lost enthusiast, pause awhile
Ere for a wild chimera of thy brain,
Thou lose this life, and lose that other too.
Ah me! It is an awful thing to die —
To leave this bright and breathing world, and go
Who shall say whither?
Who has returned from that far distant bourne
To tell us of his wanderings? who can say
He ever saw a spirit? when man quits
This mortal clay we feel it cold, and dead;
The blood that warmly ran in every vein
Diffusing life and vigour, health and joy
Is stagnant then, all sense and motion gone.
The clay machine is there; its power destroyed
The vital spark has fled; but how? and whither?
Is there an eye has ever marked its track?
Is there an ear has ever heard its sound?
Recoiling Nature points to death's last spoils
And o'er corruption pity throws a veil.

Egeria.

The hand that made this weak, and fragile form
From earthly matter, can bring back its spirit,
Which, though undying, still eludes our sense.
That hand from foul corruption can restore
The form it gave and make the dead arise.
Did we create ourselves? It cannot be;
And even your philosophers allow
A great primeval and creative Cause.
It then the Power that made us be divine
It to create be more than to renew,
We wait but his command to live again,
And that command has now gone forth indeed.

Ask of me where the parted spirit dwells
And I am dumb; but all within me cries
There is a God: He made me what I am,
He planted in my heart prophetic yearnings
For life immortal; and his word revealed
With strong assurance stamps that augury.
And now I go to death as to my bridal.
I have been rear'd in luxury, nurs'd in joy,
The child of love, and beauty — I have past
Some years of girlhood loving and beloved.
Hope led the dancing hours, and fond desire
Followed her footsteps scattering fragrant flowers.
Must not that Faith be true, that Faith be strong
Which casts aside these dearest joys of life,
And welcomes death mid tortures and contempt?

Marcus Sempronius.

It is a superstition vain, and false,
Not reason that directs thee: thou art sway'd
By artful men, who mark'd thee for their prey.
If true thy visions of a future state,
Can duteous love deserve its fiery woes,
Or filial disobedience win its joys?
Think of thy parents, of Cornelius think.
Live my Egeria, live again for love,
For thy Cornelius. Noble, hapless youth,
I saw him struck by sorrow to the ground:
His head bowed down upon his manly breast,
While the big tears upon his mantle fell.
I spoke to him, he heeded not my words,
So deeply plunged in misery — thou the cause.
Call back that noble youth while yet thou canst,
Oh! call him back to life, to Rome, to thee.

Egeria.

Ah! say no more or I am lost indeed.
Conspire not thou with all the envious Powers
To make me quite unworthy of thy name.
Oh side not with my weakness, or I strive
Against my worser nature all in vain.
Again I cling to life, again fear death.
Yet will I wrestle with grim-visaged death:
Nor shall his marrowless arms hurl down my soul,
If the all-conquering wrestler gird me still.
Let me retire: I hear Cornelius' voice
And I must struggle as I die, alone.

Enter CORNELIUS.

Cornelius.

My own Egeria wherefore shouldst thou start,
And shun me thus? Am I become thy bane,
And is my presence hateful? Then farewell!
I will begone — but ah! my will is powerless,
And thou art far too beautiful to dic.
I hear thy sister's voice, unhappy sister,
She comes to plead for me, to plead for all.
Yes we will rescue thee: the priests are near
And claim their victim for the unpitying Gods.

Enter JULIA.

Julia.

Egeria, much-loved sister, still unmoved!
Obdurate still! Here let me cling and die
Of sorrow at thy feet: — die with our mother
Who sends me here and pleads with thee in me.
Alas! To-morrow, if thou scorn to hear
The voice of nature, thou thyself must die.

Think of our happy childhood, our twin life,
Our hopeful future: wilt thou blight them all?
And shall I never, never see thee more?
Still let me hold thee, press thee in my arms.
Oh! I will strain my eyes with this fond look.
I must not lose thee, no I cannot part.
Say but one word — oh! be not so unkind
To me the playmate of thy childish hours.

Egeria.

Sweet sister, kill me not with weeping thus,
Nor heave these bitter sighs, nor cling around me.
Oh Heaven assist me now: I fear no more
The wheel, the stake. This woe overmasters me.
Oh! do not tempt me, make me not forsworn.
Sweet Julia love me less, or love my soul
More than thou lov'st this perishing outward form.
That soul immortal, blissful, will survive
Even yon orb of day that lights the shame
Of this sin-ruined and condemnéd world,
A rheum, a fever, in a few short hours
Shall kill this little life, dissolve this frame
That ye would buy at cost of all my bliss.
After some bitter tears, some natural grief
I should be quite forgotten, or should live
Shrined in calm memories of the waning past.
And now when, yearning for assuréd bliss,
I heed not some brief hours of doubtful life
Ye break my heart with grief, hang round my knees,
And drag me downward from the heaven I seek.
My sweetest Julia! My true sister, leave me,
Oh leave me for my Mother! Comfort her,
Sustain her in this sorrow: she needs all

Thy care and tenderness: — my Father too —
And let my love for them be strong in thine.

Julia.

Cornelius come; join thou thy voice, thy tears
With mine, nor rise until she grant our prayer.
Thy sister, uncle, bridegroom, kneel before thee.
Scornst thou, obdurate! Thine own Julia's anguish?
Thy Julia, once so treasured and carest?
And thy betrothed Cornelius — scornst thou him?
Hast thou no blessing for thy heart's first love,
No word of comfort for thy sorrowing kindred,
No offering to appease the offended Gods?

Egeria.

I am not stern: — 'tis Heaven, who reads my heart,
In mercy sends me strength to bear these woes.
To thee my Julia I will say no more:
Thou know'st thy griefs sit heavy on my soul.
Oh would I could avert those griefs from thee.
And thou Cornelius! Since thou will'st it so,
Hear my heart's truth, and let us part in peace.
That I have loved thee fondly thou know'st well,
That I do fondly love thee I avow.
We two grew up together in one home.
Our thoughts, our joys, our sorrows still were shared.
I saw thee beauteous, truthful, kind and brave;
And the child's fondness is the woman's love.
Oh! More than Father, Mother, Sister, dear;
Dearest — sole object of my passionate love,
When I am gone, think not unkindly of me,
As of the cruel cause of lifelong pain.
Think on Egeria as on one who loved thee
More than all Earth, and only less than Heaven:
One who is still thy bride — if thou reject not

Her proffered bridal troth. I go to Heaven
To plead for thee my sometime-sainted spouse,
Here on thy noble brow the cross I trace,
Heaven grant thee with that cross its saving grace.

Exit EGERIA.

END OF ACT THE THIRD.

ACT THE FOURTH.

SCENE I.

A street.

Enter Cornelius and Theotimus.

Theotimus.

Unhappy youth! delay thy hasty steps:
For she thou seek'st perchance e'en now is led,
A willing victim, to a cruel death.
— Wouldst thou then view her tortures? feast thine eyes
Upon the dying pangs of one so late
Soul of thy soul, and treasure of thy heart?
Hold back, hold back! thou deem'st me cold and harsh,
But I would spare thee this unnatural sight:
— Or may it move thy soul, through wondering love,
To bear thy cross like her, like her to die?

Cornelius.

To die, old man — to die? it shall not be.
So young, so innocent! — her life depends
Upon thy breath, behold I bend to thee.
To thee, a Jew, the haughty Roman bends.
Cornelius kneels to thee to save her life.
Bid her recant, and I will worship thee.
My fortune, honours, — all I have, is thine.
Give but Egeria, give me back my bride.

Theotimus.

Bid her recant? ah, little dost thou know
Mistaken, generous youth, how small my power!
Speak I God's truth which I am charged withal? —

4

Egeria listens to my every word
With meek respect, and sweet, submissive awe:
But speak I from myself, dare I to breathe
One word of baseness or apostasy? —
The Christian maid revolted at my guilt,
Shall spurn me from her presence, loathe my sight;
And all her former awe be changed to scorn.
That thou dost love her, I full well believe:
And yet to spare her some brief throes of pain,
Thou wouldst consign her to eternal death.
Thou canst not save her life at such a cost?
Retrace thy footsteps, to thy home return.
Or — wilt thou witness her triumphant death,
And learn to suffer from a Christian maid?

Cornelius.

I can nor stay, nor go. Hark Theotimus,
What sounds are these? ah! see the savage throng
Already rushing to behold her fate.
Egeria! My Egeria! lost for aye.
And shall I gaze upon that exquisite form
Exposed, and tortured: shall I see those lips
Turn pale and quiver that so oft have breathed
The words of love and comfort to my soul:
Those eyes grow dim in death? it may not be.
Theotimus hold. Oh! let me die with her.
Teach me with her to smile on shame and torture,
And gird me with her faith, her hope, her strength.

Theotimus.

Go then my son and see this martyr'd maid,
Meekly yet firmly meet her cruel doom.
Her faith, her strength, herself shall then be thine,
Yea thine for ever in the realms of bliss.

What but the certainty of things unseen
Could give her strength to bear these agonies?
Nor think it is her nature, — well thou knowst
She is not what she was few months ago,
Weak and irresolute and full of doubts.
How often has she wept, and prayed for strength,
How often has she urged her love for thee,
Her father's wrath, her mother's grief and tears,
The world's contempt, the loss of friends and fame?
Yes, I have seen her bend with streaming eyes,
And clasp her hands in agony of grief,
And beg me to avert the dreaded hour:
And I, thou deem'st severe, I wept with her.
I could not answer, but I raised my hand,
Pointed to Heaven, and knelt by her in prayer.

Cornelius.

Thy words are sword-thrusts, and they search my soul
With pangs and fears and hopes unfelt before.
Almost I would I were a christian too.
But now farewell: see! how the crowds rush on
To glut their wolfish eyes with human blood:
Hark to the savage cries of brutal joy!
"The Christians to the lions"! Out alas!
Egeria dies — old man! preserve her life:
Bid her recant, or I will plunge my sword
Into thy cruel bosom — save her life.

Theotimus.

Talk not of life, for what is life to me
Without a friend, — an exile from my home?
Is my hour come? Then do I bless the hand
That bids me leave a world of pain and sin,
For Heaven's unruffled peace, and endless joy.

Cornelius.

Away, away! I would not take thy life —
But I am reckles, I despise and loathe
The sight of man, — of thee thou cruel Greek.
My fame, my country, all to me are nought —
I save Egeria, or I die the death.

Theotimus.

Go generous youth, behold the glorious maid.
I know not if I prophesy aright,
But something tells me that thy hour is come:
That Angels tune their bright immortal harps
To celebrate a soul just freed from sin.
Sure 'tis the voice of Heaven bids me divine
That rescued soul Cornelius is thine.

Excunt CORNELIUS and THEOTIMUS.

SCENE II.

The Flavian Amphitheatre.

The Prefect, Senators of Rome, Lictors, Soldiers, People. — EGERIA is brought on the Arena and her fetters struck off.

Prefect.

Come forth young maiden, to deny the charge
That brings thee to this court — thou art accused
Of impious treason to thy country's Gods,
Of sacrilege, and superstitious rites.
And yet it cannot be the charge is true.
I gaze upon that form of youth and grace,
Those soul-revealing eyes, those truthful lips,
And may not deem thou art so false a thing.
Come maiden, boldly speak, disprove the tale,
Art thou a Christian? quick deny such shame.

Egeria.

Father! I thank thee that thou strengthenest me,
Pardoning my life of blindness: grant me now
To bear, through death, firm witness to thy truth.
Romans and friends! I am content to die.
The sense of wrong, the fear of shame and torture
Are passing from me, and my heart fills fast
With love and with goodwill to all my kind.
The coming world hath cast its day-spring on me,
Brightening to fulness of a blessed future;
And all my griefs are swallowed up in joy.
Yet oh my countrymen! How yearns my spirit
To extend this new-found bliss to all I love,
To every Roman, every human soul.
Ye who bewail me, weep not for my fate:
None happier can betide a child of man
Than thus to die for God and for his truth.
But this ye see not now: — soldiers of Christ
Hereafter, 'neath his banner ye shall fall,
Conquering no earthly kingdom by your death.
And ye who thirst in blindness for my blood,
Deeming ye do Heaven service, may that Heaven
Now hear me and forgive you. Guards lead on:
I am a Christian: for that faith I die.

The Prefect.

Let the loud clarion sound, the Flamen comes.
Thou wilt not still reject thy country's Gods.
— One trial more. See here the altar rise,
And thou must worship there, or else thou diest.
Repent young maiden, and deny thy God.

A wooden platform appears upon the Arena; in the centre an Altar with all the appurtenances of sacrifice, and surmounted on one side by a statue of Jupiter, then enter the Priests of Jupiter, and a milk-white steer is led on the Arena.

The Prefect.

Thou hast not bent thy knee, nor bowed thy head
Young maiden, to the Altars of our Gods.
The incense rises, peals the solemn chaunt
To Jove, great Jove, the King of Gods and Men.
Tremble rash renegade while Mercy lives.
At sight of thee Justice would fain relent.
But, if thy hardihosd provoke the wrath
Of this offended multitude again,
I cannot save thy life, and thou must die
A vile apostate's death within the hour.

A PAUSE.

The Prefect.

Be not so proud in wrong, unsay thy guilt,
And offer incense to the angry Gods.

Egeria.

I am a Christian, for that faith I die.

The Prefect.

Silence, nor with thy blasphemy profane
The Gods who have endured thy crime too long,
Here, take her hence, by tortures try to bring
Conviction to her wayward, impious heart.
But if she still persists, if all is vain,
Since so she wills it, let her meet her fate.
Slaves do your office, and convey her hence
And let the games and festal sports begin.

SCENE III.

Sempronius' villa.

Sempronius seated. — Enter Marcia, and Marcus Sempronius.

Marcia.

See how unmoved and stern Sempronius sits,
Wrapped in his mantle, speechless, motionless.
Thus ever hath he sat, since first our child
Was borne across our threshold from his arms.
Pride, in his soul, fights with great grief of heart.
Arise mine honoured Lord. Oh speak to me,
See here thy brother — ah! he heeds us not.

Marcus Sempronius.

Behold thy noble partner, how she bears
With majesty her sorrow, though bereaved
Of that dear child at once our love and shame.
She is a mother, and thou canst not know,
Altho' thou lov'st thy daughter as thyself,
A mother's feelings: if there be a heart
Where love unselfish, deep, and changeless dwells
Free from all human dross, full alchemized,
It is the heart within a mother's breast.
Yet with what majesty she veils her grief
For that lost, guilty, still-beloved child.
But thine is wounded pride at the contempt
This recreant daughter brings upon our name.
Look on thy favourite Julia, hear her prayer,
And bear thy grief as a Sempronius should.

Enter Julia.

Marcia.

Go to thy father child, and bid him wake
From that dim trance of anguish; bid him rise:
Alas! he heids no more his Marcia's voice.

Julia.

My honoured sire, behold thy Julia kneels,
Speak but one word, let not thy wrath increase
The awful desolation of our house.
Poor lost Egeria! Ah! dear father think
Where now she is; — and wilt thou not arise
To seek our noble Emperor, plead her cause?
Surely Sempronius will not plead in vain:
And if a father can forsake his child,
Who shall defend her, or preserve from death
The once loved daughter? Fly to save her life.
Oh! by the dear remembrance of thy boy,
Thy little Caius, — rise, and save a child.

Sempronius rises.

Who speaks that word? Julia! Was't thou that named him?
I warn thee name him not, or thou shalt wish
Thou hadst been dumb as the untimely grave
Where lies my darling boy. My son! my son!
Leave me to seek his tomb, and there in peace
Let me sit down and on the stony earth
Weep the departed glory of my race.

Exit Sempronius.

Marcia.

Follow him Marcus. ah! his reason staggers:
But let him not perceive ye watch his steps.

Exit Marcus Sempronius.

Marcia.

Stay with me here, my sole remaining child,

And let me lean on thee. See Victor comes,
How wild he looks, how pale and sad his face!
Alas! he brings no tidings save of death.

Enter Cornelius.

Marcia.

Speak noble Victor, tell us of the worst.

Cornelius.

I saw her sacred and retiring beauty
— Oh! 'twas a sight to make the sternest weep —
Led forth unveiled before that brutal throng.
At first she seemed astonished, and looked round
With hurried glances, shrinking from their gaze.
But soon collected, with a placid brow
She stood, in majesty of fearless truth,
A visible glory circling round her head;
And all eyes fell, and the fierce roar was hushed.
Calmly she heard the threats of torturing death,
Turned calmly from the proffered sacrifice,
And, when at length she spoke, these were her words
— Words which alone I will remember now —
I am a Christian: for that faith I die.
Then sounded loud the fatal voice of doom,
And she was hurried forth: yet still unchanged,
Save when her eye in parting fell on me:
Oh then her cheek grew paler than before,
And for a while a dimness was between us.
Then ran a surging murmur through the crowd,
For one so young, so beautiful, so brave,
Untimely doomed to die a felon's death.
But, with stern voice and majesty of hand,
The Prefect quelled that uproar: — she was gone.
My tale is told: I go to die with her.

SCENE IV.

A Court belonging to the Prison.

Enter EGERIA supported by Slaves followed by CORNELIUS.

Egeria.

Art thou Cornelius? Let me hear thy voice.
The veil of death is falling o'er mine eyes.

Cornelius.

And is it thus Egeria that I see thee?
That pale, wan face, that bosom stained with blood,
And this cold hand, damp with the dews of death.
Ah murdered innocent! Ah bruiséd lily,
Drooping and fading on thy broken stem!
Heroic Witness for the truth of God!
Untimely done to death by violent hands;
I will avenge thy wrongs: — Yet anger dies
In reverence, love and pity, when I see thee
Thus dying and thus conquering. Leave her slaves
To breathe away her soul within these arms.
Let satiate Justice now give place to Mercy:
Humanity is still a Roman boast.

Exeunt Slaves.

Egeria.

Am I again in these dear loving arms?
Hast thou forgiven me Victor that I leave thee?
My soul, already on its wing to Heaven,
Delays awhile arrested by thy breath.
Oh! let my wearied head recline at ease
Upon thy shoulder, let my feeble limbs
Find short repose from suffering, stayed by thee.

Look on me: — when we parted last, Cornelius,
I bade thee leave me; then my pulse beat high,
With love, and fondness for this poor poor world:
A thousand blandishments allured my soul:
Despite of all my faith, and all my hopes,
I could inspire, and feel an earthly passion:
But now that passion in thy heart and mine
Dies with the beauty that it fed upon.
Quenched is the sometime lustre of mine eye,
My lips are pale, and every grace is fled.
But now, Cornelius, a far holier love
Hath bound in one for aye thy spirit and mine.
Therefore securely in thine arms I sink,
And on thy lips breathe forth my dying sighs.
And oh, My husband! by that earlier fondness,
By all the passionate vows we two have breathed,
And by this nobler, deathless love, I charge thee
Resist not thou the Truth for which I die:
— How shall I more commend to thee that Truth?
The love I bore thee once was worldly, selfish:
Such as our idol Deities inspire.
But now I love thee with so pure a flame
That God alone is more beloved than thou.
Yield to His will through me. I grasp thine hand,
The skies are opening, rays of purest light
Pour down upon us; pitying angels stoop
To raise thy soul with mine, my Christian spouse.

Cornelius.

Inspired Persuader! If my sighs and tears
Be proofs that thou hast conquered, claim them all.
Yes, mould me as thou wilt; it cannot be
That falsehood breathes from those heaven-uttering lips.
But live Egeria, do not leave me thus.

Thy God shall be my God, thy Faith be mine;
And I will live for thee, or die for Him.

Egeria.

Oh! I am sick, and faint, perhaps 'tis joy.
But still support me, press me to thy heart,
And let its warmth revive me to rejoice
Awhile in certainty of new-found bliss.
Thou art a Christian! When within the tomb
I lie in peace, oh! come and whisper there,
Thou art a Christian. Let thy flowing tears
Bedew the holy flower I planted there,
In fond anticipation of this hour.
Farewell, farewell! sustain me or I fall.
Within thy arms I die, a Christian spouse.

She dies.

Cornelius.

Art thou gone first! Egeria speak again!
Return and hear the words thou yearn'st to hear.
I am a Christian: — put me to the proof.

Enter the Prefect FLAMINIUS and Soldiers.

Cornelius.

Barbarians! look upon this murdered saint.
Inhuman wretches, instruments of ill,
Go to your Tyrants, boast this deed of blood;
And say from me Cornelius waits them here.

Flaminius.

Distracted man, is then thy judgment warpt,
And has the loss of that enthusiast girl
Unstrung thy constant spirit? Rouse thyself,
And be the Roman thou art wont to be.

Cornelius.

Were I that Roman, thou mightst rue thy part
In this remorseless deed: but I have learnt

Her lore, and thou art safe: she hath forgiven,
And I forgive: remains the easier task
To suffer as she suffered: mine her words,
I am a Christian: for that faith I die.

Flaminius.

Away with him to prison — then to death.
This Galilæan pestilence spreads fast,
And needs the knife and brand: yet who can wonder,
When beauty's lips utter the magic words
That lead our youth astray? The charm is strong:
Witness the constancy in that pale face.
She died; and in his arms she smiled at death.
— The Nazarene has conquered: let us hence.

END OF ACT THE FOURTH.

ACT THE FIFTH.

SCENE I.

Sempronius' Villa.

Enter Marcus Sempronius, and Julia. — Marcia sleeping.

Julia.

Step gently uncle. See my mother sleeps.
Worn out with the long strife of agony
At length she slumbers. What a moan was there!
And see her outstretched arms. Sleep hath no balm
For that poor o'erwrought heart. Kind heaven assist me,
Or I shall die and leave her in her woes.
So wouldst not thou, Oh! loved and lost; to thee
How sacred was the hallowed name of mother.
She bade me watch her, tend her — oft she said:
"The child who can desert an aged parent,
Or blight the days of those who gave her birth,
Will ne'er a joyful wife, or mother prove,
The Gods will shower no blessings on her head".
But see she sobs, she starts, she clasps her hands,
Awake, awake, dear mother, 'tis a dream.

Marcia.

I saw her bleeding, give me back my child,
The lost, the guilty, I will have her back.
What would ye with her? let her rest in peace
Within her mother's arms, that cheek reclined
Against the bosom where she once reposed.

Oh! let her breathe her last where first she drew
The springs of life. Oh! give me back my child.

Marcus Sempronius.

Thy child — ah name her not, condemn'd and lost!
Cornelius is in fetters for her sake.
I saw him pass, he raised his hands and cried:
"These are the nuptial bonds I have desired,
They bind me to her with an iron grasp
And make her mine through all eternity:
For I too am a Christian: — then I felt
A virtuous anger rising in my breast.
Away, away! I cried, I lov'd thee once,
Thou wert the pride of every Roman heart,
So brave, so beauteous, so renowned in arms,
But now a base, deceiving, crouching Jew,
I spit on thee, and loathe thy very sight.
He spoke no word and silently passed on.
But oh! his look is stampt upon my brain,
And I could curse my base reviling tongue.

Enter a Slave.

Slave.

I come the harbinger of dismal news:
Our Lord is dead: no sooner did he hear
Of her who died so shamefully disgraced,
Than on his sword he fell. His noble soul
To the Elysian fields has sped its way
To seek the son he loved, and lost so soon.

Marcia.

Another shaft! Ye pierce me to the quick.
Widowed, and childless! Yet my tears are scorched:
Would I could turn to stone, and feel no more.

Julia.

My mother!
Thou totterest, and thy face is deadly pale:
Mine honoured mother; let me lead thee hence.

Marcia.

Out alas! That sound
Comes deep and hollow from a new-made grave.
Even as the voice that I no more may hear.
Ah me! Thy voice, thy very look is hers.
Oh! I can weep, — my daughter still is here.

SCENE II.

A Prison.

Cornelius.

My brain is reeling, and my strength is gone,
I am exhausted by this agony.
Tortured again, I may retract in blindness.
Come to my aid Egeria, or I fall.

Enter **Theotimus.**

Egeria's spirit sends me to this spot,
I come my friend, I hasten to thine aid:
I come to tell thee that thy prayers are heard.
Thou hast been sharply tried, and it is done.
A moment's patience and the prize is thine;
And all thy mortal sufferings are o'er.

Cornelius.

Theotimus! is it then thy friendly arm
That holds my dying head? and at this hour
When by my natural friends deserted, scorn'd,
Bereft of all I loved: thou holy man
Whom my unhallow'd lips once dared insult,
It is thy hand alone that gives me aid.

Thou saidst I should repent: the hour is come.
I hear Egeria's voice: she calls me hence.
My native, my beloved Rome! farewell!
Thy glory once was dearest, still is dear:
And though alas! I quit thee in thy rage,
Stained with the blood of martyrs, and of saints,
Thou mayst not wholly fall: thy noble sons
Shall hail the Truth on these eternal hills,
And Christian worship rise from Pagan shrines.

Theotimus.

Bless thee my son, and blessed be this hour
When Heaven's clear light hath reached thy suffering soul.
Warrior of Rome, thou wilt not fear to die:
Soldier of Christ, thou canst rejoice in death.
Oh that the great Apostle's burning words
Were mine, to unfold the mysteries of our Faith,
And turn thy Persecutors' hearts to Christ.
But His ways are not ours: some souls He wins
By living words, and some by life and death.

Cornelius.

Thy words like dew from Heaven refresh my soul.
And now bright world, loved Rome, a last farewell!
Farewell my kindred and co-mates in arms,
The joy of battle and the voice of Fame.
Commend me to those dearest left on earth,
The uncle of Egeria and her sire;
And pray them should foul slander blot my name
To vindicate our noble house from shame.

Enter a CENTURION.

Centurion.

Hast thou retracted? for the sword of justice
Already is suspended o'er thy head.

Cornelius.

Take then thy victim: bear these mangled limbs,
To torture them again. Just Heaven! I bow
My head, and worship thy divine decrees.
I die a Christian glorying in the name.

Theotimus.

Thou art indeed a Christian. Noble spirit,
Thy task is bravely done, thy trial o'er.
Eternity now opens on thy sight.
Egeria beckons thee to realms of bliss.

Cornelius.

Egeria, thou hast saved me. I am thine.
Even now mine eyes behold thee heavenly fair.
Thy form, divinely human, was not given
To bloom one moment and for aye to fade.
Corruption shall not triumph o'er thy cheek,
Nor strong Death quench the lustre of thine eye.
I come to sleep with thee the dreamless sleep.
Soon shall we wake in Glory, soon arise,
To sleep no more, in realms of endless bliss.
Give me thy blessing, Father, and farewell.

Theotimus.

Heaven's blessing rest with mine upon thy heart,
Oh fearless sufferer in the cause of Christ.

Exit THEOTIMUS.

Enter JAILER.

Jailer.

Thy latest hour is come: the guards await thee.

Enter CENTURION.

Centurion.

Stand off, stand off, and leave your prisoner free.
Marcus Sempronius comes with his reprieve.

Exeunt CENTURION and the JAILER.

Enter Marcus Sempronius.

Marcus Sempronius.

Unhappy youth deserted by mankind,
See, in thy utmost need thou art not left
To call in vain upon thy lying Gods.
Marcus Sempronius will not leave his friend.
Despite thy guilt I come: so throw thou off
Thy strong delusion. I would now discharge
My former debt to thee, and save thy life;
Since mine I owe to thy undaunted hand.
Oh, reverence again thy country's Gods!
And take the pardon that I bring with me,
Redeeming thee from ignominious death.
Or, if thine obstinate spirit will not yield,
Here is a sword, to save at least thine honour,
And free thee, by a Roman deed, from shame.

Cornelius.

Thou art the same Sempronius; and I love thee.
— The unhappy prisoner, the degraded Jew
Doth thank thee for the proffer of his life.
But can it be that one thou holdest dear
Should barter for that life his inmost truth?
A delicate maiden taught me how to die;
And can I purchase life at such a rate?
Thus then I tear and trample on my shame.

Marcus Sempronius.

Thou wilt not wisely live, — then bravely die:
Not by the arena's rabble hunted down,
But nobly, freely, as befits thy name,
Fall here upon the sword before mine eyes.

Cornelius.

Put up thy sword, and keep it for the cause
Of Rome and Justice. So to die were now

In me a coward's act. Who gave this life,
Alone may take it back: — or shall Christ's soldier
Betray his standard and desert his post?

Marcus Sempronius.

There is a dauntless spirit in thine eye
That binds me to thee — I would save thy life —
Speak but one word, or let me vouch for thee,
And say thou dost retract: — if it be known,
Then let me bear the bitter penalty.
My son, my son! preserve thy precious life;
For love, for duty, for the Gods, for Rome —

Cornelius.

Here let me kneel, and humbly raise my hands
To Heaven, and pray for thee, thou kind old man!
Honour and love be thine; and may the Power
That now directs me turn the hardened heart
Of him who on the shrines of Demon Gods
Pours forth the blood of martyrs and of saints.
Oh then at length may thy great heart be filled
With knowledge of that Truth which leads to Bliss!
— For me through death, for thee through life and joy.

Marcus Sempronius.

Blaspheme no more the Gods, or I must leave thee.
— And yet thou art too goodly and too young
In darkness and alone to wait the hour
When furious beasts shall rend thee limb from limb.

Cornelius.

Did not Egeria die, the young, the fair?
Did she recant? Could torture move her soul?
I saw that snowy bosom stained with blood:
I closed those eyes where shone the light of love:
I heard her last breath witness to the Truth:
I felt the latest pressure of her hand,

Which, clasped in minè could point the road to Heaven.
— Shall I — a man — fear dying more than she?

Enter a Centurion.

Centurion.

Cornelius Victor, we must take you hence,
The Prefect waits, the signal trumpet sounds.

Marcus Sempronius.

Must thou then die? And is my debt unpaid?
And shall the arena gloat upon thy shame?
And wilt thou take from me no boon but this?
Here 's to that noble heart! die Christian! die.

He stabs Cornelius who falls.

Cornelius.

Thy Roman mercy by that stroke hath freed me.
My blood flows fast, and with it ebbs the tide.
Of earth's poor life. But oh! what splendour streams
Upon mine inward eye from yon deep heaven.
How is that wondrous, far-retiring aisle,
With all the intricate traceries of its vault,
Illumined by the glow of costliest gems,
Emerald and opal, chrysolite and sapphire;
And, brighter than the restless diamond-blaze,
Brighter than glories of the midday sun,
A thronéd Form Divine — 'tis He, 'tis He!
Who died and is alive, who lives to save;
He whom, through death, I shall behold and live.
See, circling round that throne, on the curved front
Of an innumerous host from all the Tribes
Kindreds and Families of Heaven and Earth,
Flaming more dimly, rearward, every way,
Stand forth the Heroes of the Realm of God,
Glorious in shape and substance: — Patriarchs,

Prophets, and crownéd Kings; Apostles, Martyrs
— Oh true Egeria! — Now they close around
The golden margin of a hyaline sea
Tempering the uncreate Glory in its mirror:
They bow themselves, and cast before His throne
The starry cinctures of their radiant brows.
Now issues forth in mitigated brightness
From that unutterable light, a troop
White-robéd, wingéd, crowned with amaranth,
And waving shadowy palms: — see! see! they move
Adown the pearl-paved vista: nearer, nearer,
The martyr-legion comes. Who leads the van,
Holding another palm, another crown?
'Tis she! — I come Egeria.

Dies.

THE END.

TRANSLATIONS FROM GOETHE

&c.

BY THE EDITOR.

STANZAS

PREFIXED TO THE FAUST.

Again ye float before me, hovering Forms!
As 'erst ye gleamed upon my troubled glance.
Still do I strive to grasp with eager arms
The loved illusions of mine early trance?
Nearer ye throng! — 'tis well, if lifeblood warms
The cloudborn shapes that weave your mystic dance.
Bathed in the magic breathings of your train
My bosom feels the gush of youthful life again.

With you come dreams of many a frolick day,
And rises many a much-loved shade around.
Like dying echoes of some ancient lay
First-Love and Friendship breathe from out the ground.
All fresh comes Sorrow; nor apart may stay
Plaints for life's course in mazy error bound:
Sighs for the good, who, by the beauteous light
Of Fortune's smiles misled, have vanished from my sight.

They cannot listen to my closing strain
The souls for whom mine earlier verse I sang.
'Tis scattered now for me that friendly train,
The echo spent which once so clearly rang.
To unknown crowds I seem to sing in vain:
Nor hear I their applause without a pang:
For all who then delighted in my lay,
If yet indeed they live, are wandering far away.

There seizes me a long-unwonted yearning
For yon still realm of disembodied sprites.
My faltering voice, its tones no more discerning,
Æolian murmurings pours in fitful flights.
A shuddering thrills me: tears on tears are burning:
The stern heart in its strength no more delights.
The world around me wanes to nothingness,
And vanished things for me a real life possess.

STANZAS

PREFIXED TO A VOLUME OF SONGS &C.

The morning came; her stealing foot-steps scared
The slumbers wherein lightly bound I lay.
From my still cot, awakened, forth I fared,
And up the mount with fresh soul held my way.
Still as I clomb new joys their heads upreared,
At each new flower embossed with dewy spray:
Up rose the young day on my ravished sight,
And all things for mine own delighting breathed delight.

But soon from out the mead-embracing river
A wreathéd mist streamed forth all silently:
Varying it spread, o'er me at length to hover,
And round my head in whirls did upward fly.
That faery scene no more might I discover,
The dim grey veil had blotted every joy.
Above, beneath me, rushed the billowy flood,
And I was prisoned there in twilight solitude.

Now seemed the sun to pierce the volleying haze;
Its gloom was lightened by his struggling beam;
Its eddies drifted here in downward maze,
There split in climbing around crag and stream.
Oh! how I longed to greet the outspringing rays
Which from that troublous sea would freshlier gleam.
Long doubtful hung the airy victory;
Then burst on me the flash, and closed my dazzled eye.

But soon mine aching orbs again to bare
An inward impulse did my heart embolden:
Yet only hurried glances might I dare,
So had that blaze in glory all things molten:
When lo! borne towards me through the cloudy air
A female form was to mine eyes unfolden:
Never on earth saw I her beauty's peer:
She fixed on me her gaze, and floating lingered near.

Know'st thou me not? she cried, and in the sound
Gushed the full choral tones of truth and love:
Know'st thou me not, who many a deep life-wound
Of thine to heal my charméd numbers wove?
Thou know'st me well: — in an eternal bond
Closer to clasp me thy heart ever strove.
I marked the hot tears of thy passionate anguish,
When even in boyhood thou for me didst languish.

Ah yes! I cried, and sank in deep delight
Down on the earth, — 'twas thine that long-hid feeling:
'Twas thou didst calm me when the restless might
Of passion thro' my youthful veins was wheeling:
Thine was the heavenly plumage fanning light
My brow, in sultry noon, with coolest healing.

Earth's gifts thou gav'st me — gav'st whate'er was best,
And now, through thee alone, will I in all be blest.

I name thee not: full oft by many a voice,
I hear thee named and called by each his own:
Fain would each eye in thy pure light rejoice;
Few eyes unharmed that light may gaze upon.
Ah! while I erred, of playmates had I choice;
Now that I know thee, I am all alone:
Alone I must enjoy my happiness,
And hide and guard within the sacred fount of bliss.

She smiled on me: thou seest how wise, she said,
How needful 'twas but little to reveal.
Scarce from that fond illusion art thou freed,
Scarce lord e'en now of childhood's wayward will;
Yet deem'st thyself in wondrous powers arrayed,
And lingerest man's prime duties to fulfil.
How far dwell'st thou from all mankind apart?
Live with the world in peace, discerning what thou art.

Pardon! I cried; my aim was still for good;
And shall thy glories vainly on me shine?
A joyous spirit lives within my blood;
I know the full worth of each gift of thine.
No more the entrusted talent shall be hid:
For others blooms in me the power divine.
Why with deep longing have I yearned to know thee,
If to my brethren I may never shew thee?

Even while I spoke, her heavenly eyes revealed
A look of kind indulgent sympathy:

Myself I read there, wherein I had failed,
In what done right, while I lived wanderingly.
She smiled again — already was I healed.
Then rose my soul to unknown extasy:
Then could I first with inmost confidence
Press near to her and dwell upon her answering glance.

Now stretched she forth her hand into the wreath
Of shadowy cloud and vapour floating round:
Still, as she grasped and gathered it, beneath
Her grasp it waned and might no more be found.
Again mine eye could sweep the downward heath:
I looked toward heaven, — clear was the blue profound.
Only a veil most pure her hands did hold,
It streamed round her and swelled in many a mazy fold.

I know thee, and I know thy weaker fear:
I know the good that in thee lives and glows:
— She said, her voice yet dwells upon mine ear —
Take the long-destined gift my love bestows.
Happy is he and freed from earthly care
Whose soul receives this boon in calm repose,
Of sunlight wov'n and mist of morning's youth,
The veil of Poesy from out the hand of Truth.

And when the sultry spell of noon hath bound
Thy friends and thee, then wave it in the sky:
Cool evening breezes soon shall whisper round,
And from each blossom balmy odours sigh:
Earth's wailing passions breathe with stillier sound;
The grave shall seem a cloud-spread couch on high;
Each gently-murmuring wave of life break lighter,
The day be lovelier and the night be brighter.

Come then, my friends, and if upon your way
Full heavily life's weary load should press;
And if with golden fruits and flowerets gay
The bubbling fount of song your path may bless;
Together we will meet the coming day,
So will we live, and so life's wrongs redress;
And thus too when o'er us our children mourn,
For their delight our love shall still undying burn.

BID ME NOT SPEAK.

Bid me not speak! Bid me be still!
'Tis Duty my heart's secret hides.
Full fain to thee would I reveal
Mine inmost soul; but Fate forbids.

The circling Sun at his predestined hour
Dispels dark night and bursts in glory forth:
The rugged Cliff unlocks his bosom's store,
Nor envies one deep hidden fount to earth.

On Friendship's breast the mourner comfort finds;
There may his gushing sorrows ebb and die.
My lips a vow in chains of silence binds;
And none may loose them but a Deity.

FRAGMENT.

It may not be, it may not be,
Though angel-mildness bids me speak;
Mute is the soul of Poesy,
Faltering the voice, the hand is weak.

I dare not call thine image forth,
Where hid within my heart it lies:
In silence to thy untold worth
That heart be still a sacrifice.

There deep beyond all earthly woes
Or joys it thrills that master feeling:
There strong the darkling current flows,
And shuns the gairish days revealing.

Thy beauty is a sacred thing
Seen but in part by mortal sight;
Which harps of Paradise might sing,
And Angels gaze on with delight.

Yet o'er its fond imaginings
Of thy most fair and gentle nature
All loveliness my spirit flings
Of inward Form and outward feature.

I may not wake with airy finger
Tones echoing thy harmonious youth:
Yet Beauty mid the chords will linger
And Love still breathe the voice of Truth.

For though all-dazzled by the veil
Which earth's perfections weave around thee,
Love, who can higher beauty feel,
Hath pierced that mystic veil and found thee.

— Hath found, nor yet hath wholly won thee:
'Tis but in moods of purest feeling
That Form of brightness flashes on me,
Through pale encircling glories stealing.

'Tis when my heart too fondly dreaming
That thine with mine responsive beats: —
Ah then in heavenly lustre beaming
My tearful gaze the vision meets.

Bathed in the radiance round thee flowing
My spirit thrills with new delight:
In warmth and light each sense is glowing:
'Tis Love's own warmth, 'tis Love's own light.

And see! that brightness subtly tender
O'er Nature sheds a magic hue.
Illumined by its growing splendour
Heaven wears a purer livelier blue.

And Earth no longer sadly sleeping
In cold Obstruction's withering arms,
Swift into joyous life is leaping,
With countless wealth of kindling charms.

And human souls are bursting thro'
The bonds of Hate which 'erst had bound them.
'Tis Love's warm breath to kindly dew
Hath thawed the ice-chains clinging round them.

From mine own bosom's depth there springs
An all-unwonted gush of gladness:
I start from dreams of formless things,
Dim sights of woe, drear sounds of sadness.

That circling atmosphere of joy
With soul and sense is sweetly blending,
Chasing unrest and earth's annoy,
And still its blissful waves extending

Till every nerve in harmony
With Nature's soul the soul of Love,
Her unveiled beauties may descry,
Her low sweet accents fondly prove.

Foretaste of Heaven! but can the sprite
Stand coldly by Heaven's opening door;
Catch one glimpse of the realms of light,
Feel one blest gale, nor sigh for more?

Can he that closing portal see,
That portal closed on every hope;
Then turn him to his misery
And darkling round his prison grope?

And shall no desperate energy
Struggle from out that living tomb;
No voice wrung forth by anguish cry
Spare, spare the intolerable doom?

But will that breast of gentleness,
Heaven's loveliest symbol here below,
— Will that dear voice attuned to bless
Speak the harsh doom of cureless woe?

Will it one moment grant the wretch
To feed on Hope's ambrosial breath;
Then on the rack of anguish stretch,
And yield him to despair and death?

Oh! not for thee the barbarous skill
With cruel purpose to be kind;
Despair's fierce pang with rapture's thrill,
Warm life with dull cold death to bind.

Forgive the dark injurious dream,
Spirit of spotless purity:
Thou wilt not, canst not make me deem
Aught of thy truth unworthy thee.

I will be calm, though all should share
What one alone can rightly prize:
Thy gentle words all hearts shall cheer,
Thy smile of sunlight glad all eyes.

I can be calm — if all may bask
And sun them in thine equal eye —
But oh! the fearful, hopeless task
To curb mine inward agony,

When for an instant flashes thro'
My brain, the rending, searing thought
That to deep vows thou art untrue,
To voiceless vows too deep for aught

Of word or sigh or burning tear,
— That on another thou canst bend
That love-fraught glance to me so dear,
— That on another thou canst spend

The cherished wealth of lingering years
Laid up with thee — my treasured bliss,
Canst quench Love's wavering hopes and fears
In rayless sorrow's dim abyss.

Hence fearful thought! I may not bear
With brain unwrencht that frenzying strife:
Begone! or raging fiercelier there
Choke all the bubbling springs of life.

'Tis past! And soothing visions rise
With thy dear image on my soul: —
Visions which clinging Faith shall prize
And yield me to their mild controul.

It shall be that wild Nature's charms
Have won thine earliest fondest vows.
She folds thee in her jealous arms,
She fears the rival in the spouse.

Perchance in heavenly Love may die
Each tenderer thought of earth's affection:
Even here thy soul would soar on high,
And spring to clasp divine perfection.

— Or dost thou dwell as suns afar,
Dimly the worlds they wield discerning?
— Or art thou as the angels are,
Impassive to each mortal yearning?

Yet oh! bethink thee Love was given
For this, that self might powerless prove:
For this to passion's glow was driven,
That self might be absorbed in Love.

Bethink thee that the heavenward flight
From earth on earthly wings must rise;
That borne from Love's sky-tinctured height
On Love's bright plumes we reach the skies.

TO —

Such loveliness can Nature frame,
Yet leave her work to fade and die?
And shall our hearts not dare to blame
Rash Nature's prodigality?

Injurious thought! That form and face
Too near perfection for decay,
From sleep scarce borrowing heightened grace,
Shall bloom in Heaven's eternal day.

GÖTZ OF THE IRON HAND.

Why should I see my little son
And sain him ere I die?
He needs my blessing not, for he
Is holier than I.

VISION.

Beautiful girl! Here let me bask and gaze
On the soul's sunshine glancing thro' thine eye;
On the smooth delicate sheen of that fair cheek,
Where the faint rose-hue struggles with the snow,
Nor yet withdraws its vermeil-tinctured blush.
Rich are the full waves of thine auburn hair;
And through its glossy clusters mellowed shines
Thy clear white forehead. Down thine ivory neck
One tress escaping, in the sunlight gleams
A ringlet of pale gold. Sighing I gaze,
And my soul drinks thy finished loveliness.
Thy graceful form is bending still before me:
Still the light step and the heart's innocent laugh
Throb on mine ear —

LOVE A LANDSCAPE-PAINTER.

Once I sat upon a peak at dawning
Poring long and darkling on the mist,
Till it seemed a grey dead-coloured canvass
Hiding all things with its ample skreen.

Came a boy and sat him down beside me:
Gentle friend, he said to me, how canst thou
Gaze so listlessly on that dim blank?
Hast thou lost in shaping and in limning
All delight for ever and for aye?

On the child I looked, and murmured inly
Can that baby ever make a master?

Wilt thou then sit dull and idle always,
Said the boy, — can nought be hit off bravely?
See! I'll paint thee presently a picture,
Teach thee too some pretty thing to paint.

Scolding thus he stretcht out his fore-finger
— Glowing red it was as any rose —
Towards that woof so grey and widely spreading,
And with pointed finger-tip 'gan drawing:

First above, a beauteous sun he painted;
On mine eyes full dazzlingly it shone:
Then the skirts o'the clouds he made all golden,
And with slanting beams he pierced them thro':
Painted next the tender airy summits
Of the freshly living trees, — the hills too
Each beyond the other free retiring:
Nor beneath might watery gleams be wanting;
There a rill he led so true to Nature,
That it seemed to glitter in the sun-light,
That it seemed to babble past its margin.

Ah! fair flowers grew beside the water,
Colours too there were upon the meadow,
Blos'my blue and purple and a gold-green,
Gorgeous all like carbuncles or emeralds.
Of a sheeny azure was his heaven,
And the sky-bathed mountains far within it:
So that I beside myself and ravished
Viewed the picture now, and now the painter.

Have I then, he smiling said, convinced you
I too am a brother of the craft?
Yet the hardest part remains to finish.

Then, with cunning finger and most thoughtful
Baby-brow, again he plied his work.
Where the grove just opened on the meadow,
Where the sun-light glancingly rebounded,
There he drew the loved and lovely maiden;
Fair her form and choice was her adornment,
Fresh her cheek beneath her auburn hair;
And that cheek was of the self-same colour
As the dimpled finger that had formed it.

Wondrous boy! then cried I, what a master
In his school hath trained thee up and taught thee:
That so quick and naturally all things
Deftly thou beginn'st and well dost finish.

Whilst I thus was speaking, lo! there stirreth
In the grove a breeze its tops that waveth,
Crispeth every ripple on the runlet,
Fills the veil of that most perfect maiden,
And — what me much-wondering more astonisht,
See! her foot the beauteous maiden moveth,
Steps indeed, and walks, and nearer comes to
Where I sat beside my roguish teacher.

Then around 'gan all things freely moving,
Trees and stream and flowers and the flowing
Veil and graceful foot of the most fair one.
Did I still sit calmly on that summit,
Duller than the rock itself and colder?

FOR THE FLY-LEAF OF A MUSIC-BOOK.

Ladye! should these favoured lays
E'er again appear before thee,
Seat thee by the thrilling keys,
Where thy friend hath oft hung o'er thee.

Lightly let the prelude ring,
Lightly glance within the book;
Read no word, but ever sing,
— Thine the tone and mine the look.

Ah! how dead these songs appear
From thy soul of music parted:
Through those lips their melody
Makes me blest or broken-hearted.

FROM THE FAUST.

Scene: — A narrow Gothic chamber with high and dark vaultings; the mouldering walls covered with skeletons; presses in the corners heaped with old mathematical instruments and other learned lumber.

Mephistopheles, who has unawares subjected himself to Faust's power, and who is now his prisoner, presents him, by the aid of certain ministering spirits, with a dreamlike succession of images, in unison with Faust's own secret longings for deliverance from the pangs of solitary incommunicable knowledge, and for a full enjoyment of all the living influences of nature. The imagery mingles with and forms Faust's dream: Mephistopheles having lulled him into a magic slumber, escapes. —

Vanish! ye gloomy
Overhead vaultings!
Let the delicious,
Life-giving blue sky
Lovingly glance in!
Were but the cloudy
Canopy cloven,
Small stars are twinkling
Softly, and milder
Suns beaming through.
Children of heavenly race,
Spiritual Brightnesses,
Bowing down graciously,
Pass stately on.
Streaming forth after them
Many a longing wish
Outward is gone.
With garments fluttering light
Richly the land is dight,
Richly the bowers,
Where, in deep earnestness,
Lovers to lovers pledge
Life-long devotedness.
Bower by bower see!
Thick-sprouting tendrils!
Clusters hung heavily
Fall in the teeming vat
Of the red wine-press:
Swiftly in rivulets
Gush forth the foamy wines,
Murmur mid pure gems,
Leave the high terraced hills
Lying behind them:

Spread themselves out in lakes,
Bathe in deep pleasure
Green slopes and flowery knolls.
Birds skim there twitteringly,
Sipping delight;
Glancing against the sun,
Glancing against the bright
Blossomy islets,
Which on the waves float
In magical heavings;
Whence we hear chorusses
Lustily carolled forth,
Where on the verdant meads
Dancers we see,
Who mid free breezes dis-
-Sport themselves joyously.
Some from the uplands are
Momently gleaming;
Some on the shiny lake
Frolicsome swimming or
Floating in air.
All to the soul of life,
All to the infinite
Depths of the loving stars,
Offering each his own
Homage of bliss.

FROM THE FAUST.

Scene: Margaret's room — Faust alone.

Hail softest twilight! through this shrine
With shadowy gloom thy glimmerings interweaving:
Seize all my heart, thou exquisite love-pain!
On dews of hope still pining still reviving.
How breathes around the soul of stillness,
Of order and of deep content!
Amid such poverty what fulness!
What bliss in such imprisonment!

He throws himself into an antique chair.

Oh take me thou that many a race bygone
In joy and grief hast held with outspread arms!
How oft of yore to this paternal throne
Have clung and clustered round the infant swarms!
Perchance too, thankful for that hallowed Christ,
My Love here nestling, her full childly cheek
Upon her grandsire's wrinkled hand hath pressed
With pious joy and gentle kisses meek.
Maiden! I feel thy spirit's breathings reach me,
Spirit of order and pure housewifery,
Which like a mother day by day doth teach thee
To spread the table with fair napery,
And on the clean floor strow the crackling sand.
Of fairest, dearest heavenliest hand!
With thee a hut were heaven indeed — And here!

He draws aside the bed-curtain.

What sudden extasy thrills through me! Here
Whole hours might I muse away.
Here, Nature! mid thy light dreams formed

The household angel grew; here lay
The child, her tender bosom warmed
With panting life, and here, by purest workings,
God's holy image did unfold itself.

OPENING OF THE TASSO.

The scene is at Belriguardo, a country-house of the Duke of Ferrara's, in a part of the garden adorned with busts of the Epic Poets — Virgil's nearest on the right, Ariosto's on the left.

Leonora, Princess of Este.

Thou look'st upon me smiling, Eleonora,
And look'st upon thyself and smil'st again.
What moves thee? Let thy friend the secret share:
Thine eye is pensive, yet thy smile is glad.

Leonora Sanvitale.

I own, my Princess, that well-pleased I see
Us both here decked out in this country guise.
Methinks we seem right-happy shepherdesses,
And busied as such happy ones should be
In weaving coronals: This, gay with flowers
Swells ever more and more beneath my hands:
Thou hast, with higher aim and mightier heart,
On the soft wavy laurel fixed thy choice.

Princess.

The leafy sprays which thoughtfully I wove
Have found themselves full soon a worthy head:
On Virgil, grateful, do I place my wreath.

Leonora.

And I my full and lusty chaplet bind
On Master Ludovico's lofty brow.
He whose sweet sports of fancy faded never
May well have portion with the budding spring.
'Twas by my brother kindly done to bring us
Thus early to the woods and fields again.
Where we may be our own, and hour by hour
Dream ourselves in the poet's golden age.
Dear Belriguardo! Here full many a day
Of my youth's prime have I lived joyously.
And now this fresh green and this cheering sun
Bring back the feeling of that time again.

Princess.

Yes, 'tis a new world that surrounds us here,
The shadows of these ever-verdant trees
Already become grateful, and already
The murmuring of the stream refreshes us.
The young sprays wanton in the morning breeze.
With innocent childlike eyes the opening flowers
From out their beds peep lovingly upon us.
The confident gardener opes his orangery;
The blue heaven rests in quietness above;
And on the horizon's verge, in softening mist,
The snow of the far mountains fades away.

FROM THE TASSO.

THE POET.

His eye but glances on this Earth, his ear
Drinks deeply in the harmony of Nature.
Whate'er old Story yields, what Life presents,
Freely and lovingly his heart receives.
The fragmentary can his mind unite;
His feeling can endow with life the lifeless.
He oft ennobles what to us seems common;
And what men prize to him is nothing worth.
In this his proper magic circle wanders
The wondrous man, and leads us spell-bound on
With him to wander, and to share his being.
He seems to approach us, yet he dwells apart:
He seems to gaze on us, but spirits may
Strangely usurp for him our corporal presence.

A noble spirit to no narrow circle
Can owe his building up — his country, then,
The world must work upon him: glory and blame
Both must he learn to endure; so best compelled
Rightly to know himself and know his kind.
Enemies will not, and friends may not spare him.
The struggling youth thus brings out every power,
Finds what he is and feels himself a man.

A talent forms itself in quietness,
A character i'the main stream of the world.

FOR A VERY YOUNG & LIVELY LADY'S ALBUM.

CAPRICCIO PER REGALARE UNA CREATURA.

La Barbarina ha un certo non so che.

Now all poetic curses
Light upon Album verses!
They 've set me here to praise thee.
'Twould much amaze thee,
And little please thee;
I'd rather tease thee,
Play with thee, walk with thee,
Stay with thee, talk with thee
Nay — frown not — kiss thee.
When thou 'rt away, I miss thee.
When thou art near me,
Dear me!
How merrily
My heart goes!
How cheerily
The time flows!
Every thing's couleur de rose.
How is this?
In sooth I know not how it is.
Let us see:
Though thou art pretty,
Some there are prettier:
Though thou art witty,
Some there are wittier:

French, Italian, canst thou sing
And canst make the swift keys ring
With martial notes that upward spring
Joyously.
But some are more Italianized sicuro,
And may be cleverer at a bravura.
Yet when before me,
How is it that these clever, handsome, witty people
bore me?
And if they stay
Away
For ever,
I wish them back never.
How is this?
In sooth I know not how it is.

TO MINNIE —.

On being asked to contribute to her illuminated Album.

Fayre Boke, of faerie Chayne together holden!
Sweete Flowers of Wytte, inne sylken Leaves enfolden!
What darynge Spryghte shalle Blondel's Harte embolden
To proffere Drosse, where alle arounde is golden?

Notte hys, bryghte Dyes to spredde with conynge Fynger:
Notte here, o'er Lai of hys, bryghte Eyne may lynger:
One onelye Offerynge hadde he skylled to brynge her:
Butte ah! — She lysteth notte the Minne-synger.

ALBUM VERSES

FOR E. M. S.

On her accusing the author of having a simile for every-thing.

Muses of Greta's Castaly!
Your aid a suppliant deeply needeth,
Who hath for all things similes,
No simile for peerless Edith.

Roused by your softly-beaming eyes
And gentle smiles, glad Fancy' springs
From out her darksome cell, to drink
The beauty of all beauteous things.

First spell-bound by that Parian stone
So sweetly bending heavenly fair,
Lingering she broods o'er Arno's banks
And fondly breathes Etrurian air.

She glances up the track of years,
To dwell in rapture and amaze
Where Sophoclean life inspires
Calm purity, majestic grace.

But marble is a soul-less thing
And statues gleam in ghastly beauty,
Condemned for aye to loneliness,
To know nor home nor love nor duty.

And Fancy tho' delighted turns
From moonlit scenes thus coldly bright,
And craves unsatisfied the play
Of social feeling's sunny light.

Let then thine image dwell with me
Enshrined in holier recollections;
Round thee shall cluster sportive dreams
Of homefelt joys and kind affections.

Yet might it wake one transient smile
Or chase one thought of shadowy hue,
A thousand fleeting likenesses
Would start to pay thee homage due.

A couching Fawn, an Antelope
Up-bounding from turf lightly prest,
A Chamois mid Helvetia's rocks,
A Swan by Derwent's wave carest:

— A Saxon Ladye shalt thou be
Distributing to all their bread,
Even as we saw thee self-forgot
Within that faery torrent's bed.

If still thine own loved Derwent please,
— A slight Birch o'er his streamlet bending,
— That streamlet's murmuring lapse, all joys
Of sound and sight harmonious blending.

And Derwent's flood, though voluble,
Can rest in pools of amber clearness,
Can gaze on Heaven's delicious blue,
Can give Heaven back in tenderer dearness.

LINES

for an Album presented to Mary Doria by Omar Effendi, on his final departure from England for the East, through Italy.

Mary! — for severing seas between us foam
Dimming the flush of scorn, emboldening shame —
On that thy household and familiar name
Which breathes the sweetness of an English home
And thine its gentle inmate, let me dwell
In fondness Mary once, ere yet I sigh farewell.

Thy home is of the West. The genial light
Of pure affection, and her kindling smile
Warm not our hearths: our hearths alas the while
Are chill and mirk; are quenched in blood; or bright
With an unhallowed lustre, fiercely burn:
Such thoughts are not for thee, — gladly away I turn.

And thou wilt pity: — but I would not so
Be pitied. Othman's son can meet his fate
With heart not manned as erst by Pride or Hate:
By tenderer feelings mine is strengthened now;
And still thy Name shall be the wondrous spell
With softening, calming power that inborn pride to quell.

And hath it fall'n so soon to this weak wailing,
This brooding o'er the Doria's twofold Name,
Each fatal to my lineage? — One, the same
Before whose orient star the crescent paling
And glimmering sinks e'en now: Andréa bore
The other: — tell his deeds thou red Ægæan shore!

Yet, for thy sake, I go to tread alone
The proud pavilions which in Genoa rose,
At that stern Doria's bidding, to repose
His arm from slaughter on my kindred done:
Then, a sad pilgrim, seek those Roman halls
Where Beauty and thy Name hallow the glowing walls.

Take, Mary Doria, take my last farewell!
And give — thou wilt not more — this shadowy boon
Thy Name and Memory: As the queenly Moon
Envies not to the wreathéd ocean-swell
Her train of glory o'er his darkling tide,
Though safe within that track the homeward skiff should glide.

"I HAD A DREAM" — FRAGMENT.

"I had a dream which was not all a dream:"
Methought I stood within the time-worn towers
Of that grey castle which o'erlooks the vale
My boyhood loved — the distant chime of bells
Came varying with the breeze: a sense of home
Was in the sound, a thousand thronging fancies
Of that dear home forth-peeping thro' its hood,
Moss-rose and starry jasmine, on a world
Of tangled wilderness and luxury
Of leaves, flowers, fruitage — the lush Eglantine,
With glossy sprout and deep retiring bell,
Where the bee sucks and slumbers, Hyacinths
Kissing whose full-formed buds poor Zephyr faints

In panting languishment, proud Tiger-Lilies,
Bedropped with moles of deepest crimson, Poppies
Flaunting i'the sun and overtopping flowers
Of rarest odour and retiring grace: —
As thee fair slender Lily of the Vale
Still canopied in tent of watery green,
And all too chary of thy delicate breath.

THE CHANGING DREAM.

Her locks besprent with April showers,
Her eye with glee and pleasure dancing,
Her heart's redundant gladsomeness
Through dimpled laughter flashing, glancing -

Alas for human weal and woe!
That sparkling eye is dimmed by weeping;
That sunny cheek now cold and pale,
Sorrow's perpetual dews are steeping.

Ah joy! she breathes again of youth; .
Tho' tempered its once dazzling brightness:
Her blush again is eloquence,
Her heart and step are bounding lightness.

CLIFDEN.

Sweet Clifden! O'er thy glassy pool
The drooping ash is fondly bending,
And in thy tranquil delicate bowl
All summer hues are Faeries blending.

Full purely through thy chrystal glows
Each dark green holly's glossy leaves,
Save where the aspen's paly stem
That mimic grove descending cleaves.

Still o'er the moss-grown natural rock
Thy welling waters idly dash,
Still fondly drinks my dreaming soul
The tinkling chime and sleepy plash.

VOTUM.

To be redeemed from self, to be devoted
Heart, soul and body to a worthy object,
To love and to be loved: — this is to live:
And whoso dwells in this forgetfulness
Of self, is holy, happy, blessed and blessing.
But we are selfish and soul-darkened men: —
Know not our proper good, or knowing it
Are slow to grasp and impotent to hold.

Oh for an Angel's insight, to discern
At once our duty! — For an Angel's strength
To plunge at once in self-abandonment,
Nought fearing, doubting nought: to find our lives
There where we throw them from us: but if this
Be yet too hard; if yet the bloodhound self
Dog our resolves and growling drag them backward;
Then gracious Heaven! train us in thy love,
In thy deep wisdom and unbounded power,
Upward to this high freedom. May our lives
Be one continued striving to this end.
May we for this be quickened to discern
The Good, the Beautiful, the Holy: — all
Footsteps of thy pervading Spirit, still
Itself unseen —

TO THE SUN — Fragment.

Thou visible emblem of Eternity
And of its great Inhabitant, permit
That I regard thee — He who creating thee
Created all things double, poured upon thee
Excess of glory, that thou mightest answer
To Him alone of things invisible.
Come, let me scan thee, and in thee discover
Some portion of thine Author's excellence;
Some shadowy image of unspoken glory,
Glory unspeakable and unconceived.
Well did that ancient Magian and the Gebir

With thine own incense and with burning heart,
Worship and bow before thee: — thee his God
Or the shrine worthiest his Divinity.
Without thee what were all things? All this frame
With thee so lovely, so instinct with beauty:
— The purple ice-peak and the evening sky
Azure and gold, vermilion, ruby, sapphire,
Emerald: — or if aught richer the swart mine
Or orient Fancy lends: — deep-blooming Summer
Spring's paly green, and Autumn's nut-brown richness
Nay Winter throned within the dropping caves
Of deep blue glaciers, owe to thee their all
Of beautiful and grand: — soul-stirring sights
Wildering emotions, which from out their breasts
Do pluck men's spirits. But is Beauty all
Thy beams awaken on this rude cold earth,
This darkling ball of blind and rayless matter?
Laughs the glad cornfield in the cold moon-beam?
Or does the sailing Pine refresh his branches
In Summer's Light alone? 'Tis Summer's Heat
Which gives the drooping ear its golden hue,
Which fills with lusty juice the fruitful vine,
Which decks with leafy wreaths the graceful Ash,
And with the strength of ages ribs the oak:
Hail genial Heat! Mysterious source of Life
Next to the general Parent. Without thee
Light were a niggard boon —

ON HEARING THE TYROLESE BROTHERS.

Oh strange delight! Again in Switzerland!
Surely from some deep-cloven sunless glen,
Or from some buttress of the beetling Glacier,
Issues this wondrous and unearthly sound:
And with it comes all fresh the intense delight
Of that loved region: — the enormous Alp
Clothed in sweet pasturage: — green flowery slopes,
Breathing of thymy odours, herd-besprinkled:
Below, brown stream-indented hills, above,
Rocks musical with that same din — a voice
Which the pleased Echoes toss from crag to crag,
Unequal as themselves: a freeborn strain,
Joyous, exulting: yet an undersong
Of no unpleasing melancholy steals
At intervals upon the listening ear.
Heard once it is a feeling evermore.

GARDEN ECLOGUE.

Nightingale.

Silly mortal, pensive mortal, wherefore dream'st thou
here alone?
Can my music soothe thy sadness, my complainings
mate thy moan?
Hast thou left thy loved one lonely; pines she too and
dreams of thee?
Or is thine the sadness only, her's a joyous heart and
free?

Mortal.

Friendly Minstrel, gentle Poet, thou my sorrow canst not
know:
Thy sweet language may not shew it: 'twill not in thy
numbers flow.
Natural moods of grief and gladness pour thou forth
in liquid strains:
Leave to us capricious sadness, leave us self-inflicted
pains.
Our true hearts no coldness severs; ebbs not there
Love's gushing tide:
Past for both all proud endeavours fond affection's truth
to hide.
Thou canst mourn thy mate departed, thou canst wail
thy nest betrayed:
Then thy plaints are broken-hearted, then thy moanings
pierce the glade.

But when spring with leafy screen hides and guards thy bower of love,
When with Summer's deepening green dimly glooms thy chosen grove,
When thy mate now wooed and won nestles near thy swelling heart,
Canst thou then, oh loving one! dream a cause shall bid you part?
— Part for hours of lonely sorrow, part for days and moons unblest,
Part till many a restless morrow points to hope a deeper rest.

Nightingale.

(— Here followed a burst of most eloquent, musical, and untranslatable vituperation, which at last suddenly gathered itself up into an indignant pause.)

Mortal.

Rightly hast thou deemed of folly: — true sweet minstrel was thy voice.
Sooth no more my melancholy, bid me not again rejoice.

PEACE.

The church-bells are ringing,
The nightingales singing,
The peacocks are flinging
  Their wild notes on high:

The blackbird is wooing,
The cushat dove cooing,
The swallow pursuing
  His mate thro' the sky.

The east-wind is veering,
The spring-flush appearing,
The warm summer nearing:
The proud steed careering,
Is plunging and rearing,
  In liberty bold.

Flitting o'er the broad meadow
Sunny light and swift shadow
Are glancing and glooming:
The far trees are looming
Through pearl-grey, or blooming
  In emerald and gold.

White-canvassed cloud-gallies
— No one hastes, no one dallies,
From her path no one sallies —
Over hills over vallies
Unceasingly sail:

Through a sea of bright azure,
Bathing earth in deep pleasure,
On they float in still measure,
Fraught with argosy treasure
Of wealth without fail.

Man and nature rejoice,
And with manifold voice
They proclaim their heart's choice,
And bid welcome to Peace.

And tho' fleeting each token,
Like a swift word once spoken,
Each loved image broken,
Joy of heart may not cease.

SONNET.

SWORD OF THE SPIRIT.

Sword of the Spirit! On thy two-edged blade
Are mystic Shapes of wondrous might engraven
Whose Archetypes behold the interior Heaven.
Hell saw thy withering flashes, and dismayed
Sought in his lowest depths a murkier haven.
For us have milder gleams around thee played.
Mirrored in thee, Earth's daily things are made
Severely beautiful. To thee is given,
Beyond that fabled spear, power to destroy
And power to make alive: thee God's elect
Alone may rightly wield. Marrow and joint
Spirit and soul cleaveth that searching point.
So armeth He man's hallowed Intellect
To quell His foes, and crown His friends with joy.

SONNET.

PYGMALION'S STATUE.

For heavenly Beauty and for heavenly Love
The Cyprian Sculptor yearning, broods o'er thee.
Ah dear delight he cries! Ah bounteous Jove!
Giv'st thou my breathing Work my Bride to be?
Thus Truth Divine half veiled in fancies rare
Fed Earth's sweet prime beneath Heaven's secret care.
For so the Spirit from Eternity
Yearned for the Bride, and wrought to shape her fair.
When brooded o'er the weltering Waste His Power,
First perfect Form rose from that uncouth lair;
Then felt, inbreathed by Him, the living Soul,
And quickening Spirit — latest, noblest dower.
Hark! Deep in Time strikes the forewritten hour:
The Spirit hath the Bride: — closed is the mystic scroll.

CPSIA information can be obtained
at www.ICGtesting.com
Printed in the USA
LVHW041400260123
737950LV00006B/589

9 783375 138080